Acclaim for the

"It's the author's ambition that attracts…his sense of reaching beyond our expectations of what a book like this (or, really, any book) can do…[A] triumph."
—*Los Angeles Times*

"Not content with writing one first novel like ordinary mortals, Ariel Winter has written three—and in the style of some of the most famous crime writers of all time for good measure. It's a virtuoso act of literary recreation that's both astonishingly faithful and wildly, audaciously original. One hell of a debut."
—*James Frey*

"Massive and marvelous…it's difficult not to feel a little spellbound by *The Twenty-Year Death*."
—*Washington Post*

"*The Twenty-Year Death* is a bravura debut, ingenious and assured, and a fitting tribute to the trio of illustrious ghosts who are looking—with indulgence, surely—over Ariel Winter's shoulder."
—*John Banville*

"This is audacious and astonishingly executed. What might seem at first like an amusing exercise for crime fiction buffs becomes by the end immersive, exhilarating, and revelatory."
—*Booklist*

The door from the hall crashed shut and Vee appeared in the mirror, framed by the square arch that separated the rooms. "Don't you just love it?" she said.

She was in a knee-length sable coat with a collar so big it hid her neck. She wasn't bad to look at normally, deep red hair, unmarked white skin, and what she was missing up top was made up down below. In the fur and heels she looked sumptuous.

"I hope he's planning to p— to give you more than a fancy coat."

"He's paying for the suite." She opened one side of the coat, holding the other side across her body, hiding herself. But I could see that she wasn't wearing anything underneath anyway. She slid onto the bed behind me, putting her hands on my shoulders. In the mirror, a line of pale skin cut down her front between the edges of the fur.

"He didn't wonder why you weren't staying with him?"

She faked shock, raising a hand to her mouth in the perfect oops pose. "I'm not that kind of girl," she said, and then she flopped back on the bed, her whole naked body exposed now, her arms outstretched, inviting me to cover her.

"You were just with him," I said.

"But now I want you..."

The Twenty-Year Death:
POLICE AT
THE FUNERAL

by **Ariel S. Winter**

A HARD CASE **HARD CASE CRIME** CRIME NOVEL

A HARD CASE CRIME BOOK
(HCC-108-Z)
First Hard Case Crime edition: July 2014

Published by

Titan Books
A division of Titan Publishing Group Ltd
144 Southwark Street
London SE1 0UP

in collaboration with Winterfall LLC

*This book is a work of fiction. Names, characters, places, and
incidents either are the products of the author's imagination or
are used fictitiously, and any resemblance to actual events or
persons, living or dead, is entirely coincidental.*

Print edition ISBN 978-1-78116-795-3
E-book ISBN 978-1-78116-888-2

Design direction by Max Phillips
www.maxphillips.net

Typeset by Swordsmith Productions

The name "Hard Case Crime" and the Hard Case Crime logo
are trademarks of Winterfall LLC. Hard Case Crime books are
selected and edited by Charles Ardai.

Printed in the United States of America

Visit us on the web at www.HardCaseCrime.com

in memoriam J.T. with apologies

POLICE AT THE FUNERAL

1.

I sat on the edge of the hotel bed trying to convince myself that I didn't want a drink. The argument that it had been three months since my last drink—and that had only been one Gin Rickey—and almost seven months since my last drunk wasn't very convincing. I tried the argument that I would be seeing Joe for the first time in four years, and Frank Palmer, Sr., the lawyer, and probably Great Aunt Alice too, so I should be sober when I saw them. But that was the reason I wanted a drink in the first place.

I glared at the mirror attached to the front of the bathroom door. I knew it was me only out of repeated viewing, but now, about to see my son, I saw just how broken I looked. My hair was brittle, more ash-gray than straw, and my face was lined, with crow's feet at the corners of my eyes, sunken cheeks, and broken blood vessels across the bridge of my nose. I looked worse than my father did when he died, and he was almost ten years older then than I was now.

"You don't want a drink," I said to my reflection. Then I watched as I sighed, exhaling through my nose, and my whole body sagged.

Why the hell was I back in Maryland, I asked myself, back in Calvert City?

But I knew why. It was time to pay Clotilde's private hospital again. And I owed money to Hank Auger. I owed money to Max Pearson. I owed money to Hub Gilplaine. And those were just the big amounts, the thousands of dollars. There were all kinds of other creditors that wouldn't be too happy to know I was three thousand miles from S.A. There had to be money for me in Quinn's will. Otherwise Palmer wouldn't have called me.

The door from the hall opened in the front room. It crashed shut and Vee appeared in the mirror, framed by the square arch that separated the rooms. "Don't you just love it?" she said.

She was in a knee-length sable coat with a collar so big it hid her neck. She wasn't bad to look at normally, deep red hair, unmarked white skin, and what she was missing up top was made up down below. In the fur and heels she looked sumptuous.

"It's the wrong season for that," I said.

She came forward. "He'd been saving it."

"I hope he's planning to p—to give you more than a fancy coat."

"He's paying for the suite." She opened one side of the coat, holding the other side across her body, hiding herself. But I could see that she wasn't wearing anything underneath anyway. She slid onto the bed behind me, putting her hands on my shoulders. In the mirror, a line of pale skin cut down her front between the edges of the fur.

"He didn't wonder why you weren't staying with him?"

She faked shock, raising a hand to her mouth in the perfect oops pose. "I'm not that kind of girl," she said, and then she made herself ugly by laughing, and flopped back on the bed, her whole naked body exposed now, her arms outstretched, inviting me to cover her.

"You were just with him," I said.

"But now I want you. That was just business anyway."

I shook my head, my back still to her, although I could see her in the mirror.

She dropped her arms. "What's wrong with you?"

"I want a drink," I said.

"Then have one."

"I can't."

"Forget what the doctors say." She was losing her patience. "You'd feel a lot better if you took up drinking again instead of always whining about it. Now come here. I demand you take care of me."

I looked back at her. She should have been enticing, but she was just vulgar. "I've got to go." I stood up.

"Like hell you have to go," she said, propping herself up. "You bastard. You can't leave me like this."

"The will's being read at noon. As it is I'll probably be late. That's what we're here for in the first place, remember?"

"You pimp. I'm just here to pay for you. I should have stayed with him upstairs. At least he knows he's a john, you pimp."

"If I'm a pimp, what's that make you?"

"I know what I am, you bastard. You're the one with delusions of grandeur."

I could have said, that's not what she thought when she met me, but what would be the point? I left the room, going for the door.

She yelled after me. "You'll be lucky if I'm here when you get back."

I went out into the hall. I should have left for the lawyer's before she got back. I had heard her go through that routine more times than I could count, but it was the last thing I needed this morning. No matter how much she got, she couldn't get enough. An old man couldn't satisfy a woman like that. But when I first met her, I hadn't felt old. She'd made me feel young again, and I hadn't realized what she was until later. I wasn't any pimp, I'll say that, but a man's got to eat, and she was the only one of the two of us working.

I took the elevator downstairs to the lobby. Instead of pushing through the revolving doors to the street, I went into the hotel bar. The lights were off since enough sunlight was creeping through the Venetian blinds to strike just the right atmosphere. It took my eyes a moment to adjust. When they had, I saw that I was the only person in the bar other than the bartender, who stood leaning against his counter with his arms crossed looking as though he was angry at the stools. I went up to the bar. "Gin Rickey," I said.

He pushed himself up, grabbing a glass in the same motion. He made the drink, set it on a paper doily, and stood back as if to see what would happen.

I drank the whole thing in one go. I immediately felt lightheaded, but it was a good feeling, as though all of my tension was floating away. I twirled my finger, and said, "Another one."

The bartender stood for a moment, looking at me.

"Room 514," I said. If Vee's "friend" was paying for the room, he could afford a little tab.

The bartender brought my second drink. "Don't get many early-morning drinkers," I said, picking up the glass.

"It's a bad shift," he said.

"And let me guess. You worked last night too."

"Until two ayem."

I tipped my glass to him and took a drink. He watched me like we were in the desert and I was finishing our last canteen. I set the glass down, careful about the paper doily. "If you came into big money, I mean as much money as you can imagine, what would you do with it?"

He twisted his mouth to the side in thought. Then he said, "I'd buy my own bar."

"But this was enough money so you didn't have to work again. You could settle down anywhere, or don't settle down, travel all over."

"What would I want to leave Calvert for?"

"Get a new start. You said yourself you were miserable."

"I said it was a bad shift."

"Aren't they all bad? Every last one of them."

He put his big palms down on the bar and leaned his weight on them. "No, they're not. Are you finished with that? Do you need another?"

I waved him away. "When you're a kid, you know how you dream you'll be a college football star or a fighter pilot? How come you never dream of just being satisfied?"

"I like tending bar."

"Right." I drained the last of my drink, and felt composed, at least enough for the reading of the will, even with Joe there.

"Kids don't know anything anyway," the bartender said. "What do you do, mister?"

"Nothing anymore. I was a writer."

"Anything I would have heard of?"

"Probably not," I said.

"You need another?"

I shook my head. I had a soft buzz on, and it felt good. It felt better than it should have. "Put the tip on the tab," I said. "Whatever you think's right."

"Thanks, mister."

I shrugged. "I just came into some money."

"Well, thanks."

I waved away his gratitude. It was making me feel sick.

I walked out of the bar and pushed my way through the revolving door in the lobby onto Chase Street. The August heat and humidity had me sweating before I got to George and turned south towards downtown. Calvert hadn't changed much since Quinn and I lived here in 1920. Or was it '21? The Calvert City Bank Building over on Bright Street that now dominated the skyline hadn't been there, and there had been more streetcars instead of busses, but overall the short and stocky buildings of the business district were the same. I remembered when those buildings had seemed tall, after *Encolpius* was published and I suddenly had enough money to marry Quinn. Now Quinn was dead and *Encolpius* and all my other books were out of print and even Hollywood had thrown me out and my life would never be as good as that day here in Calvert thirty years ago.

I was one poor bastard. If I had known how much of our married life was going to be screaming at each other and trying to outdo the other with lover after lover, pill after pill, drink after drink, I would have—at least I hope…yeah, I would have called it off. Quinn knew how to make me jealous from across the room. It was only natural when I started stepping out. And there were the two miscarriages and then Quinn started bringing a bottle to bed and finishing it in the morning, so of course I did the same. It got to the point where I couldn't think without something to get me going. We tried the cure, once in New Mexico, once in upstate New York, but it didn't last long, and when we got to Paris, we didn't care anymore, it was all-out war.

And then I met Clotilde. She set Quinn off more than any of the others. And when I began to sober up for her, Quinn left me. She told me I had a kid only after the divorce had gone through. Then Clotilde and I married and we were happy for a while at least, until we went to Hollywood, or maybe it was still in France… Anyway, she got famous, with thousands of men after her, and the public had forgotten me, so who could blame me when I had a girl or two on the side? No one. But Clotilde ended up in the the madhouse, and I was broke, and I borrowed from everybody who I knew even a little, and now all I had was Vee.

As I walked and felt sorry for myself, my mood sank lower and lower, and the effect of the alcohol wasn't helping it any. How could Quinn have left me any money after all these years? Maybe Joe had asked for me to be there, but had been too ashamed to contact me directly. I was his father after all. I passed the C&O Railroad building, and turned into the Key Building where the doorman, with a big servile grin, followed me inside, skipping ahead to reach the ornate brass elevators before I did. "Good morning, sir. Where are you off to?"

"Palmer, Palmer, and Crick, to see Mr. Frank Palmer the senior," I said.

He pushed the elevator call button and then pushed it again repeatedly. "May I ask your name, sir?"

"Shem Rosenkrantz. Do I need to be announced?"

His eyes flicked over, and he smiled and waved at someone who came in behind me. "Morning, Mr. Phelps."

Mr. Phelps started right for a door that must have led to the stairs. "Sam," he said with a single nod, and disappeared through the door.

Sam beamed back even as the door shut. How could a guy like that be happy, with a job pushing buttons and kissing ass? I guess some guys have to be that way, making everyone else feel bad because they feel so goddamn good. He turned his attention back to me. "Mr…"

"Shem Rosenkrantz." The sweat was streaming down my face. The hand of the floor indicator swung counter-clockwise, counting down the elevator's progress.

Then he answered my question from before. "No need to be announced. I just like to keep track of who's in the building. For security reasons."

The elevator bell rang and the heavy doors rolled back.

A man and a woman stepped off. Sam had fresh smiles. "Mr. Keating. Sally."

They smiled and nodded and hurried to the door. I started to walk around Sam to get at the elevator. He moved out of my way, nodding his head. Then he leaned into the elevator reaching around to the control panel and he hit the button for floor eight, the top floor. He gave me one last smile, and I almost told him Quinn was dead to knock that smile off his face, but I didn't. "Eighth floor," he said, and the elevator doors closed.

2.

The elevator rolled open on the eighth floor revealing the reception room of Palmer, Palmer, and Crick. The place had been redecorated since the last time I'd been there, brought into the 1950s, the walls paneled in dark hardwood, the floor a tawny deep-pile wall-to-wall carpet, and the clutch of waiting-room furniture upholstered in maroon patent leather. The two secretaries behind the high front desk wore headsets. The one on the left was talking into hers, while the one on the right offered me a professional smile.

"How may I help you?"

I stepped forward, not bothering with a return smile. It wouldn't have looked right given the occasion, and there was no use wasting it on one of those office girls. They probably got the sweet talk from the janitors on up. "I'm here for the reading of Quinn Rosenkrantz's will. Shem Rosenkrantz."

"Yes, Mr. Rosenkrantz. Mr. Palmer is in the conference room just through these doors to the right."

I drummed my hands on the top of the desk, then gave an awkward nod, and headed through the door. It had been maybe twenty years since I'd been to those offices for the divorce. Palmer's son had still been in law school then, and now he was a partner. Crick had had only four other shysters under him and half of the eighth floor instead of the whole thing. I guess some people have to come up in the world while the rest of us go down.

The conference room was poorly lit. The same paneled wood from the reception room covered the walls, with gilt-framed oil portraits of the senior partners at regular intervals along the inside wall, each lit by its own arc lamp attached to the frame. The other walls were devoted to glass-fronted bookcases with uniformly bound sets of law treatises. I felt the moment of distraction I always get in a library, the need to look at the titles, to flip through a volume, to search out my own books amidst the stacks. But I knew that these books were dry lifeless things that held no interest to anyone but lawyers, which was perhaps more interest than anyone had in my own work anymore.

"Shem, Shem, I'm glad you're here." It was Palmer Senior, now almost seventy-five, crossing the room ramrod straight with the vigor of a man half his age. He took my hand in both of his. "I'm sorry it's under these circumstances," he said, and held my hand a moment longer than was necessary, trying to be discrete about smelling for liquor on me. So what if he did?

"Mr. Palmer."

He gave my hand one more squeeze and let it go. "Frank. Please, Frank. And you look well," he said, which wasn't true. Then he stepped back and indicated the conference table. "Please, take a seat. We'll start this shortly. It won't take long."

I stepped up to the table and put my hands on the back of one of the oversized leather armchairs. There he was, Joseph and a young woman whom I took to be his fiancée, next to each other on the far side of the table. They talked in a subdued whisper, Joseph purposely ignoring me, and that hurt. It wasn't right, and it hurt.

It had been three years since he and I had spoken, four since I'd seen him at his high school graduation. He'd grown up; lanky limbs fleshed out, broader face, the hint of a beard or at least the five o'clock shadow that stood in for a beard. If I hadn't known who he was, I would have said he was one of those angry young men who want something they're never going to get and are just realizing they're never going to get it, so they're going to make the world pay for it. You see lots of those guys hanging around the corner or at the pool halls or the garage. But usually they're not sitting on a couple of million dollars like Joe.

His fiancée—I'd forgotten the name she'd given on the phone two weeks before when she called about Quinn... that she...about her dying—the fiancée was a prim blonde, with an aura of wispy down over lightly tanned and freckled skin, a soft woman with which to make a wealthy life. She hazarded a look, and when our eyes met, she smiled despite herself, and that made up for Joe some.

In the back of the room, in the corner, not even at the table, sat Connie, Great Aunt Alice's Negro maid. A stocky woman now in her late forties or early fifties, she held her large trapezoidal purse in both hands on her lap. She gave me a polite nod when I caught her eye.

"Now I've asked you all to be here," Palmer said, taking the chair at the head of the table, "because you or those you represent are mentioned in Mrs. Rosenkrantz's will in one way or another." He took a machine-rolled cigarette from a silver case and lit it with a paper match. He waved out the match and tossed it in a brass ashtray, then slid the folder on the table closer to him. He opened it, and talked down into the will, and I sat down.

"I'm going to read the will aloud straight through, and I ask that you hold any questions until the end. We can go through it line by line after that, either together or individually. I want to urge all of you, no matter what has happened in the past, not to get excited here and make any decisions. These things can take time, and there will be time enough for any unpleasantness later." He looked up at us without raising his head like a judge handing down a sentence. "Not that I expect any unpleasantness. This is a simple will, and to my infinite sorrow, there aren't many Hadleys left as you can see here today." He picked up the papers, and tapped them on end to straighten them.

Joseph sat hunched in his seat, his nostrils flared, a scowl cutting valleys that joined his nose and mouth and pushed dimples into either side of his chin. His bride, turned sideways, held his clenched fist with one hand and his forearm with the other, her entire attention on him.

Palmer started, "I, Quinn Rosenkrantz née Hadley, being of sound mind and body, do solemnly swear that this is my last will and testament signed on this Thursday the 12th of June 1941, containing instructions for the dispersal of my estate, both real and liquid, and personal effects. This will is to make null and void all previous wills and agreements…"

It went on like that for several pages, Palmer intoning

the words in a rapid-fire monotone. There was an out-
dated section regarding Joseph's custody should Quinn die
when he was still a minor. I was named fourth in line after
Quinn's grandmother Sally Hadley, who had since passed
away in '45, then Great Aunt Alice, and then Connie
Wilson, who shifted uncomfortably when that part was
read, for it was surely meant to be a jab at me.

All cash, stocks, bonds, insurance policies, and other
liquid assets—in short, somewhere around two million
dollars—were to pass into Joseph's possession if he was of
age, and into a trust overseen by Palmer and the elder
Hadley women if he was not. The house was also Joseph's.
Its contents, however, were his only after Great Aunt
Alice had selected any items of importance to her.

As Palmer had stated, a simple will. Except for this.
Should Joseph predecease Quinn, the estate would be
dispersed as described, but with me in his place.

"…pursuant to the laws of the great State of Maryland
and the United States of America. Signed, Quinn Rosenkrantz, Thursday the 12th of June 1941, witnessed by
Frank Palmer Sr. and Frank Palmer Jr., Thursday the
12th of June 1941."

Palmer cleared his throat and ran his hand across his
lips. He took a drag from his cigarette and gathered the
papers. There was a palpable and awkward silence. I was
stunned. That Quinn might award me anything had been
a shock; but that I had been in line for everything—it
emptied my mind. But then, Quinn had all the reason to
believe that Joseph would survive her. So maybe my
place as the next heir in line was meant as no more than a
gesture, a way of being the better party and lording it

over me. And this was why Palmer had gotten me all the way out from the West Coast? He should have saved me the trouble.

The silence continued. There was an understanding that the cue had to come from Joseph. He had just been awarded a tremendous amount of money. But he sat with the same scowl on his face, his eyes straight ahead, not focused on anything, no doubt fuming at my position in the will. The fiancée, Connie, and I all shifted in our seats, and Palmer cleared his throat again, which turned into a barking cough, and then he stood, picking up the folder in one hand and his cigarette in the other. I stood as well, and Joseph's gaze remained steady, now somewhere around my belt.

"My secretary can have copies available for any of you later this afternoon," Palmer said, and he walked around and put his hand on Joseph's shoulder, which elicited no reaction. He leaned down, and I heard him say, "Joe. Are you okay?"

Joe said nothing. Yeah, he was a hard boy now.

"Joe, we should talk about a will for you at some point."

Still nothing. Palmer appealed to the fiancée with his eyes, but she shook her head primly. He said, "Joe, we can do it right now, if you want, or you can set up an appointment with my secretary, but it's important you have a will."

Palmer looked across the table at me, and that woke me up, and I started to leave. As soon as I made it through the doorway, I heard Joseph say, "Not now. Maybe after we're married."

He wouldn't even talk when I was in the room, my

own son. I didn't care what he thought I had or hadn't done—and I'm not saying I hadn't done anything, because you can ask anyone, I'm the first to admit I've done something wrong—but to not even talk in front of me, that just wasn't right.

"Joe, a will…"

"When we're married," he repeated, and then I was in the reception area out of hearing range.

Palmer came out a moment later. "Shem." I turned and he shook my hand again. "I'm sorry about all of this," he said.

"Sorry about what?"

"Quinn's dying. I'm not supposed to see you people dying. You're supposed to bury me."

"I'll have someone remind you of that at my funeral."

"It was spiteful what she did about Joseph's custody. I advised her not to do it."

"It's a moot point now."

"I still wanted you to know, it wasn't the right thing to do. But you couldn't have expected to come out any better from this thing financially."

"I didn't expect to have come out at all."

"Like you didn't come out for the funeral?"

I smiled and said nothing to that. So that's why he got me out here, out of spite.

He gripped my upper arm. I could tell he smelled the alcohol on me. But so what? Can't a man have a few drinks every now and then? "She loved you still, you know."

"Thanks for thinking that."

He looked back in the room. "I'll be in my office. I'm available to you for the remainder of this hour. I'll have those copies prepared." And he strode out of the room, his cigarette perched in his mouth.

I shuffled my feet, sort of just standing there. I figured I better get a copy of the will or Vee would think I was holding out on her. In the conference room, the fiancée was leaning right into Joseph's ear. The sight caused a pang of jealousy, not so much about this particular girl, but just the idea of a girl whispering earnestly in your ear. Vee wouldn't ever have done that unless she planned on shouting next, to break your eardrums, her idea of a joke.

Connie came out of the conference room and slid up to me then, her purse still gripped two-handed and held at her waist. She nodded. "Mr. Rosenkrantz."

I forced my face to stretch into a wide, charming grin, a skill I had learned in the wilds of my youth with Quinn when charm mattered above anything else. "Connie, how long have you known me? Shem, please."

She hunched her shoulders, and backed a step away from me into the shadows of a five-foot ficus tree. "Mr. Rosenkrantz. Miss Hadley expects to see you while you're in town. You will stop by the house later?"

The last thing I wanted just then was to see Great Aunt Alice. She had a famed reputation for not pulling her punches, and in the state I was in, there were plenty of punches to throw. "Well, Connie, I don't know if I can," I said, still displaying that dapper grin.

"Tea is generally at two-thirty."

I checked my watch as a stall. Just one now. "I don't think that's going to work for me." Connie's whole body fell in disappointment, as though inviting me to tea was the real reason she was there, the reading of the will just a coincidence. "You'll send Aunt Alice my best, of course."

She took another half-step away from me. Then, "I'm sorry for your loss."

I sighed through my nose. "Thank you, Connie."

She waited another half beat and the fiancée appeared beside me, her brow wrinkled, her lips puckered ever so slightly. Connie ducked and said, "Thank you," and hurried to the elevator where she pushed the call button and watched the row of lighted numbers above the door.

I turned to the fiancée, who looked a little lost, and renewed my smile. "I'm sorry, but I don't remember your name," I said.

She looked at me, confused, as though she didn't expect that I could speak. "Yes, of course," she said, "Mary O'Brien." She held out her hand, and I took it, turning it so I could hold it in both of mine.

"Joseph is a lucky man."

She looked at her hand in mine, but seemed unsure how to reclaim it. "Yes, well…"

"I thought Quinn always wanted a daughter."

"She was very kind to me, even while she was sick."

It was hard to reconcile the phrase "very kind" with Quinn, but I nodded as though I knew just what she meant. "Perhaps we could mend things now. I would very much like to have a daughter as well."

"I thought Joe needed some time to himself," she said. She had exquisite cheekbones and small bright eyes and her unease and the wrinkle across her brow were precious.

"Of course."

"He's upset. He's not himself."

I still held her hand and it grew warm in mine. "Of course."

"I've read your books," she hurried.

I felt my own face falling, the charm slipping. "Thank you."

"Joe didn't want me to, but I needed to. You do see why? Don't you?"

I felt strained, tired.

"You will be my father-in-law, even if... Well you understand."

Joseph appeared then, still stormy, and upon seeing me clutching his future wife's hand, he sucked in his lips to try to control himself as he took her by the elbow. "Come now, Mary."

She drew her hand back as though she'd touched something hot and he steered her towards the elevator. It was a move I had used many times myself on his mother— but never on Clotilde—and I knew Mary was in for a talking-to on the way home.

"I was just saying you're a lucky man, Joseph," I said, keeping pace, but maintaining a distance of several feet. "I wish you'd give me a chance to make things right with us."

He kept his eyes on the numbers above the elevator, his back to me, not even allowing the possibility that I might come into his line of sight, and whose fault was that? My own son! He kept a firm grip on Mary's elbow. I knew my face had grown plaintive, and it made me sick at myself.

The elevator came, the bell dinged like the end of a round, and I watched them get on. Just before the doors

closed, they turned, and Joseph gave me a withering look
of pure hatred, a look that hurt more than any words
could have, used to, as my years of drunkenness had
made me, declarations of disgust, pathetic amusement,
consternation, pity, and sadness. I didn't think I'd ever be
able to pick up my feet to walk a single step. And my
empty stomach was much too hollow.

3.

I got my copy of the will and went back to the hotel. Vee was sitting in front of the vanity in her slip, making up her face. She turned in her chair when I came in. She had only done one eye so far, so the right eye looked wide and innocent while the left was hard and mean. "Well?" she said.

I threw the will onto the vanity in front of her, and sat on the bed in almost the same position I had been in that morning. "I thought you weren't going to be here when I got back."

She had snatched up the will and was skimming through it, flipping pages. "Tell me. I don't understand this stuff. What's the number?"

"Nothing."

"Nothing? What do you mean nothing?"

"Just that. I didn't get anything. It all goes to my son."

She threw the will at me. It bounced off of my arm, fell onto the bed, and then slid over the edge, fluttering to the floor. "Then why the hell did we come out here?" She turned back to the mirror on the vanity, and went to work on her other eye.

"I'm mentioned. If Joe had died before Quinn, it would have gone to me."

"Well, a lot of good that does us."

I wanted to say her anger didn't do us a lot of good

either. But why bother? She was like that. It didn't matter that I was feeling just about as if getting up to go to the bathroom was too much effort, she was laying into me.

"You better get ready to spend a long time here," she said, applying her makeup with hurried, jerky strokes. "Because you can't think I'm going to get Carlton to pay for your ticket back to S.A. You were a deadbeat loser out in Hollywood and you're a deadbeat loser on the east coast too. When will I ever learn?"

When would either of us? "You didn't think that when you met me. You threw yourself at me. You loved my books. You were a fan. It was such an honor."

"And didn't you eat it all up. I'd read some of your books. A big-time writer. I didn't know you were broke." She started putting away her brushes, gathering tubes, pencils, closing various compacts, and stowing them in her makeup kit. "All you care about is that somebody's read your damn books. Well nobody has."

She said that just to hurt me. And it worked every time. We were like a broken record, having the same fight over and over, and still each word squeezed me tighter and tighter. "Where are you going?"

"Carlton put the wife on a plane to Palm Beach this morning. It's just the two of us for the next few days." She snorted. "And you." She got up and crossed the room to the armoire on her side of the bed, and pulled out a black sheath dress. She held the hanger above her head to examine the sheer fabric.

"Are you going to be back tonight?"

She bunched up the dress to get at the hanger.

"Wouldn't you like to know?" She had the dress over her head.

My chest squeezed even tighter, and my anger turned into anxiety. I hated her one moment, and I couldn't live without her the next. "Vee, please. You've got to come home tonight. I don't know if I can take being alone."

"Then don't take it." The dress fell down the length of her body. "Go out. Go find some floozy, or go jump off a bridge, I don't care." She straightened the dress, and then turned her back to me waiting for me to zip her up.

I got up, came around the bed and gripped the zipper. "I'm serious, Vee. This thing with Joseph…" My eyes stung, and I tried to swallow the lump in my throat. "I don't have anyone anymore, and my own son…he's my own kid, and he won't even talk to me. You don't know what that's like."

"I don't even know where my kid is," she said, waving her hand over her shoulder, hurrying me.

I zipped her up. "That's different. You gave your kid away. Joseph… He wouldn't even look at me."

"You know what?" She picked up one foot and slipped on a heel, and then the other. "If he's hurting you so badly, I'll tell you what to do. Kill him. That way he's out of your hair, *and* the money is yours."

The idea was so startling that I didn't know what she meant at first. "Money?"

"From the will," she said, fully dressed now. "How do I look?"

"What are you talking about? How could you even say that?"

She rolled her eyes, and shook her head. She pulled a small black sequined purse out of the armoire, and went to the red handbag on the bed. She started pulling things out of the one and putting them into the other, her wallet, a small vial of perfume. "At least you're drinking again. Thank god for small favors." She pulled out her gun, a pearl-handled two-shooter that Carlton had given her.

"Why do you need that thing?"

"Carlton doesn't like it if I don't carry it. Where are my keys?"

"Vee, Joseph—"

"It was a joke. Relax." She threw the red handbag down. "God damn it, where are my keys?" She stood up and stared at the vanity, shook her head, and clipped her purse closed. "It doesn't matter. I don't need them anyway."

With every further preparation, my throat got drier, and the muscle in my cheek spasmed. The thought of killing Joseph made me nauseous. Vee leaving made me weak. I started thinking about what drink I would order downstairs when she left.

She expertly stormed into the living room towards the outer door.

I called after her, "I love you."

She called back without turning around. "I told you about saying that." The door opened. "It's not true anyway." The door closed behind her, and I was alone, and I couldn't figure out where to go, or how to even take a step.

What I wanted was to go down to the bar. I knew it was a bad idea, but that's what I wanted—a Gin Rickey.

It sure sounded good. But I was on the wagon again, I told myself. That morning had only been an exception. I couldn't have another drink, it was the last thing I should do.

But, I thought, maybe I could go see Joseph again. Give it another try. He might just see me. That girl of his Mary seemed open to smoothing things over, a nice girl and she liked my books. When a guy's dame got involved, anything could happen. He might… But I knew he wouldn't. I wasn't kidding myself. Joe would just see it as a grab for Quinn's money, and he'd probably be right.

The money! What was I going to do for money? We were counting on that inheritance. Vee would leave me here, she really would. There was a time when I just had to cable that I had a story written—not the story itself, just that it was written—and a magazine would cable $1000 just like that, and that was during the Depression, too. But nobody would give me money now. They couldn't even pretend it was an advance at this point. I hadn't written a single sentence in years. But if I did write…

If… Ha!

But if I did… Then they'd have to send me money, Auger or Pearson, somebody. Maybe I *should* write. That's what I could do. Then I'd get some money, and then once one story was written, I could write another, maybe even take on a novel again. There was no reason I couldn't! A publisher would love to have a new Shem Rosenkrantz book, a triumphant return.

I looked around for the pad a good hotel like the Somerset always provided. It was on the telephone stand in the living room. I picked it up, and underneath there

was a room key attached to a plastic diamond that read
"Suite 12-2." It had to be the key Vee was looking for.
Without thinking, I slid it in my pocket and began to look
around for a pencil. There wasn't one on the stand. I
opened the drawers of the desk, then both bedside tables.
There wasn't anything to write with. I even checked the
bathroom.

I stood in the center of the living room, tapping my
foot, and scanning the suite to see if there was someplace
I had missed. I could go down to the desk to get a pencil,
but that seemed like too much effort. And as I thought
further about it, I got more anxious, and the idea of
writing began to seem insurmountable. I didn't know
what to write anyway. I didn't really want to write either.

I stepped to the phone, picked up and asked for a long
distance connection to California. It took almost a full
minute, but then I was through to the Enoch White facility
on a shoddy connection. "Yes, this is Shem Rosenkrantz.
I'd like to speak to my wife." It was mid-morning in
California, and it was likely Clotilde was outside on the
grounds if the weather was nice. But it wasn't more than
two minutes until her voice came through to me, and the
connection improved.

"Shem?" she said.

I grew weary, her voice an excuse to let go. She'd make
it all better. "Clotilde…"

"Have you been drinking?" she said. Just like that.
One word and she knew.

"We didn't get anything from Quinn," I said. "We got
nothing."

There was a pause. When she spoke again, her French accent was thicker than at first. "Director Philips has been very good to us," she said. "I'm sure he'll understand."

"I'm not sure he will," I said. The director had made himself quite clear on my visit the previous week. We had to the end of the month, and then they would either release Clotilde or transfer her to a state hospital.

"But I'm Chloë Rose," she said, the name one she hadn't used in ten years. "I'm…it's good for their advertising, no?"

"I'm not sure it matters anymore."

Her voice grew tight and I started to pull myself together. I couldn't hope that she could take care of me; I had to take care of her. "I can't leave here," she said, and then switching to French, *"Je n'ai pas—"*

"English, Clotilde. My French is no good anymore."

"Shem, it's not safe for me to leave. It's just not safe."

I couldn't tell if that was a threat, that she would kill herself if forced to leave, or if it was part of her paranoia, her paralyzing fear that she was going to be attacked at any moment.

"It's not safe, Shem."

"I know, sweetheart."

"You can talk to Director Philips."

I sighed. "I will."

"Shem, I can't leave."

"Calvert's nice," I said, trying to put cheer in my voice. "You remember that time we stopped here, it must have been '36, '37, before the war? We picked up Joe?"

"Shem. Don't let them make me leave."

I forced a smile. "Don't worry, honey. It's going to be all right."

"You'll talk to Director Philips?"

"Put him on," I said, and immediately there was a clunk as she put the receiver down. She would go find a nurse who would transfer the call back to the front desk who would then transfer me to the director's office. She could never figure out how to transfer me back to the desk herself. While I waited, listening to the faint shush of the open line, I thought again about my options. Maybe I could ask Joe for a loan. He could afford it now. Or maybe Vee could get some actual cash out of this hood Carlton. My chest tightened as I ticked off each option, knowing that they weren't ever going to be.

Director Philips came on the line, all business. "Mr. Rosenkrantz."

"Director Philips, I just wanted to assure you, I'm in Calvert, things are working out, it's just going to take a little time, I'll be able to pay you some of our arrears."

"That's great news. Thank you for telling me."

"I just want to make sure there are no preparations for Mrs. Rosenkrantz to be moved. It upsets her very much."

"Of course. We know how to take care of our patients, Mr. Rosenkrantz. That's why we cost what we do. Just wire the money as soon as you get it, and there won't be any trouble."

"Of course, as soon as I get it."

"Good day."

"Yeah. Goodbye." I set down the receiver, but left my hand on it. I felt worse than before I had called. Now I really needed a drink. But first, maybe I'd call Auger or

Pearson. If I told them Clotilde was going to be thrown out… But I'd called so many times, the secretaries knew not to put me through. Maybe I could send a telegram. I hadn't asked them for money in…it had to be three months. No, it must have been more. If I told them I was writing again, maybe that would force me to actually write. It was a chance.

I threw the pad onto the couch, and went out into the hall and to the elevator.

Downstairs, I hadn't gotten two steps from the elevator when somebody said, "Mr. Rosenkrantz."

I turned. It was a young man, about twenty-five, maybe a little younger, about Joseph's age. His face was long and narrow. He wore wire frame glasses and a gray felt fedora with a red feather on the band. He was brimming with excitement, shuffling his feet as though he might have to run after me at any moment.

"I…" He started to pat his jacket. "I—if you…just one moment." Pat, pat, pat. "Here…" He reached into his inner coat pocket and came out with a pad. "If I could…"

I saw then, and I shook my head. A reporter. "I'm not interested. No comment." I headed for the front desk.

As expected, he jumped after me. "Mr. Rosenkrantz. Sir. Please. I am a reporter. I cover the city council for the *Sun*. But I just…I mean, I'm a fan. I'm a writer too—"

That was even worse. I turned, about to lay into him. I could feel it rising, and I wasn't going to be able to stop it. But he was leaning in towards me, with a stunned expression on his face, an expression I hadn't seen in a long time. And I paused. "What do you write," I said.

"Well, for the paper…"

I waved him on.

"I had a play produced last year at the Everyman. *Spook*. My first. It got some nice notices."

"And you are...how did you find me?"

He looked down as though he were ashamed of doing what reporters do. "I knew your wife's will was to be read. Your ex-wife's, excuse me. I waited outside the building where it was to be read, you understand, and when you came out—I knew it was you from the pictures on your dust jackets—I followed you, but I didn't have the guts to say anything. And I nearly didn't just now either."

"So you're a fan?"

"Yes, sir."

"What's your name?"

"Taylor Montgomery, sir."

I held out my hand. "Nice to meet you." He shook it with wide-eyed wonder. That was how it should be. That was how it was at one time. If only Joe had met me like that. I'm his father, he should have given me that look. He should have given me a hug, you know, like rough-housing, but it's a hug. "Buy me a drink," I said.

"Oh, no, really..."

"Look," I said. I was starting to feel bad for the kid. Nobody should be that paralyzed to talk to me. And suddenly everything seemed better. Of course Auger would send me money. How couldn't he? I was his client. I made him a lot of money back in the day. Yeah, he'd wire money, and then Vee would come back west with me, and it would all be okay. I might even get a $400 week at one of the studios if I begged hard enough. "Look," I said again. "You go to the bar. Order yourself a drink. I've got to send a cable, and I'll meet you in there. And if you're not there, then I understand that too."

"Oh, I'll be there," he said. "Thanks. Mr. Rosenkrantz. Yeah," and he stepped backwards, and almost tripped into somebody, said "Excuse me," righted himself, gave an embarrassed smile, and headed for the bar.

If only Joseph had met me like that. That was the way it was supposed to be. I had worshipped my father. I would never have turned my back on him, even when he said all of those horrible things about me becoming a writer. He took it all back when I sold my first book too. But Joseph shoots daggers at me, and this kid Montgomery treats me right.

I started for the front desk. A tall man in a three-piece suit said, "How can I help you, Mr. Rosenkrantz?" Don't you love that about hotels? They always make you feel important.

"I need to send a telegram."

"All right." He reached down and came up with a telegram form. "Do you need a pen?"

I waved at him impatiently, and he handed one over. I wrote Auger's name and address on the top, and then I wrote:

IN CALVERT STOP NEED MONEY STOP PLEASE WIRE $200 OR WHATEVER YOU CAN TO SOMERSET HOTEL ROOM 514 STOP

I paused for a moment, and then added:

AM WRITING AGAIN STOP I THINK I'VE REALLY GOT SOMETHING STOP

Then I crossed out that last line, reread the whole thing, and crossed out the line about writing too. I pushed it across the desk, and the deskman, who had been standing off to the side ignoring me in order to give me privacy, came alive and took the telegram and the pen.

"Charge it to the room, sir?"

I grinned. "Yes. Charge it to the room." And then I thought, if Carlton's paying for it all, I should really send one to Pearson too. Maybe the publishing house could spare a little petty cash. "Actually let me have another." I wrote out the same message, handed them both over, and then headed straight for the bar. This was good news, and it deserved a celebration. I was still on the wagon, of course. This morning's drink was for courage, and no one would begrudge me a drink to good fortune.

4.

But as I crossed the lobby, the anxiety began to creep back in. Pearson had told me never to cable him for money again. He said he didn't think he'd publish me again even if I ever wrote anything. And Auger had always been nice to me, but he would only go so far. And Vee was out with another man, and Quinn just teased me with her will to get me in a tight spot, no doubt, and Joseph wouldn't even look me in the eyes.

I went into the bar, and Montgomery was sitting on a stool near the entrance with an untouched pint of beer in front of him. He was jiggling his foot on the lower rung of his barstool. Here was a young man who had read my books. I could still reach out and touch someone half my age, younger. There was that. Maybe everything was fine, and I was just worrying for nothing. I came up behind him, put my right hand on his back and leaned into the bar. It was the same bartender from this morning. I caught his eye, and he nodded and then brought over a Gin Rickey.

"So, you're a fan," I said, taking a deep gulp from my drink.

Montgomery shrugged sheepishly, but once he started talking, he was full of passion, like I had been once, when the writing was still fun. "I read *Sweet as Summer* when I was fourteen, my uncle who lives in West Virginia gave it to me, and when I finished it the first time, I just turned it over, and read it again."

"You like that one? It didn't sell too well, but it got some good reviews."

"Yeah, I like it. But my favorite's *Only 'Til Seven*, but everyone probably says that. I've read all of your books, most of them more than once."

He was starting to come on a little strong, and he ducked his head, realizing it, but I liked hearing it anyway, so I didn't stop him. Before I knew it, I had finished my drink and the bartender was setting up another one. "So what was this…play you wrote? What'd you say it was called?"

"*Spook*."

I raised my eyebrows and circled my hand to say, come on.

"It's just about a former slave who lives over on the west side, and there's a ghost living in the house that is actually a white slave owner, and they talk about slavery, and freedom, and really everything. About being a man."

"And that's it?"

"That's it." He looked down at his beer, which he still hadn't touched. "It makes more sense when you see it."

I swallowed half of my drink, and patted him on the back again. "Drink up, drink up." He picked up his glass and took a tentative sip. "So you work for the newspaper. I was never quite able to do that. I did some reporting for a small-town paper for maybe it was a year, and that was enough for me."

"A man's got to eat."

I nodded, and drank the rest of my Gin Rickey.

"There's no money in the theater unless you make it to New York, and even then…" he said.

"Yeah?"

"You can make some real dough in the theater in New York. If you're lucky. Or you know the right people."

I waved to the bartender. "I know the right people, I think, but I'm not lucky." The bartender set down my third drink. There was a part of me that was saying I should take it slow, but there was another part of me that didn't care. "You know, I wrote a play once."

"*In Justice.*"

I frowned and nodded my head, impressed. "You *are* a fan. I didn't think anyone read me anymore."

"Sure they do."

"Who?"

He paused.

I smiled and shook my head, and then threw an arm around his shoulders. "It doesn't matter. You read me. You know *In Justice.*" It felt good to be taken seriously. I'd almost forgotten what it was like to have somebody's respect. It didn't make it all better, but it sure helped a lot. Or maybe it was only the alcohol. In either case, I felt at ease. I raised my glass. "My wife probably doesn't even know *In Justice.*"

He looked into his drink again, remembered he was supposed to be drinking it, and picked it up in both hands like it were a mug of hot cocoa, and took a sip. He knew about my books, so of course he knew about Clotilde. Everybody knew about Clotilde. I wished I hadn't brought her up.

I kneaded his shoulder, and slapped his back. "But go on, tell me. You're going to write another play."

That brought him back. "I'm working on something. It's just an idea really."

"You knew about *In Justice*," I said, shaking my head. "What do you think of that? Did you like it?"

"Oh, sure. It was great to read." He looked to see if he had insulted me. "I mean, I've never seen it done. I've only read it, but I'm sure it's great on stage too, is what I mean."

"What's the new play about?" The bartender set another drink next to the one I hadn't even finished. I guess he'd decided I was a big spender. And why not? All thanks to Carlton. Or to Vee, my girl. I pointed at Montgomery and called to the bartender, "He's on my tab too."

"Oh, thank you, Mr. Rosenkrantz. I couldn't…"

"Of course you can. We're celebrating. To my only fan." I raised my drink, and he raised his. We tapped our glasses and both drank up.

"Mr. Rosenkrantz, sir, could I maybe interview you?"

"Maybe later, kid. Your editor wouldn't want to run it anyway. Besides, I thought you said you were on the city desk."

He shrugged.

"What's this new play about?"

He took another drink. Now he was loosening up. And it was about time, since I already felt as though I couldn't stand. "It's called *The Furies*, and it's based on this story I did a little ways back, about a family out in the county, a mom and her three kids. Her husband, if he was her husband, had run off. Her little boy got hit by a tractor one day, crushed his leg, but when she went to the hospital they kept taking other people and so she went home, but the leg rotted and the kid died. So she went back to the hospital with her other two kids and she cut their throats one after the other right there in the emergency room, saying that it was no different than what they'd done to her little boy."

"That's all true?"

"All up to the killing her other kids. I embellished it a little. The one kid died though."

I shook my head. "Nah. No, you can't kill two kids on stage like that. No one would come. No one would put it on. What if she's about to kill them and the action stops and the Furies, the actual Furies from the myths came down, and…"

He was leaning forward on his stool. "And what?"

"I don't know maybe they take her around and show her it's wrong."

"Like *A Christmas Carol*?"

"I don't know. It's your play. You write it. You don't have to listen to advice from a washed-up old man like me."

"No, I like it. The Furies come down, they take her to—"

"Isaac on the rock," I said, and punctuated it with a drink. I was sweaty now, that uncomfortable hot feeling that makes you sick to your stomach.

Montgomery was looking at me even more amazed than when he first found me. "You wouldn't…I mean, you must only be in town…you wouldn't want to write this play with me?"

"No, son, no, you don't want to do that."

He leaned forward. "I do."

I considered him. Having a young, hungry, energetic writer alongside of me might be just what I needed to get me going again. I wished I'd left the sentence about the writing on the telegrams after all, because I could see it might just work. It wouldn't even take long, no more than a week in all likelihood. Hell, I must have written a dozen screenplays in less than a week.

I slapped him on the back and pulled him close, my arm around his neck, stopping just short of tousling his hair—a man didn't deserve that kind of disrespect no matter how young he was. I held onto him to prevent me from keeling over, and said, "Why don't we give it a try? Who the hell knows, maybe we'll get something. At least we'll have a few laughs."

He went to his pocket and produced the reporter's pad he had brought out before and a fountain pen, and he started to write. "So they go to Isaac on the rock." He looked up. "Wait, how do the pagan Furies get to the Old Testament?"

"Once the Furies come in, the audience is either with us or not, so what does it matter if we mix and match a little."

He could see I was right, so he nodded, and started writing, and I started talking and it just came out of me. I don't know how, but on and on, the two of us throwing ideas back and forth, the bartender setting up drinks, and Montgomery was drinking right alongside me now. We were matching each other drink for drink—he'd switched to rum and Coke—and from what I could tell, he could hold his liquor. I reached that familiar plateau where my mind focused, and my body let go, and some of my best work was in that state. No, all of my best work was in that state. Inebriation. What a wonderful word.

And it wasn't just me. Montgomery also. He really had an ear for dialogue. I'd just need to suggest a scene, and in no time, he had it all marked out, and the characters sounded just as natural as we were talking. Every now and then I thought, I should stop drinking. I needed to go to bed. I needed to find some way to get out of here tomorrow. But the idea of the empty hotel room, of what Vee was up to, was too much, and I knew I shouldn't be alone. This thing with Joseph would start to eat me up if I went upstairs alone. So we kept talking, fleshing it out. And who could blame me if I kept tossing down the drinks. I was in a bar after all. What did anyone expect?

After a while, I started to notice that Montgomery was slowing down, and was a little green in the gills, hanging over the bar like all he could think about was keeping his head up. And his eyes kept darting to the clock behind the bar. Of course it was ten minutes fast, but that didn't change that it was almost eight o'clock and we'd been there nearly six hours.

"Son," I said, patting him on the back. "It's time for us to recess. We can resume our composition tomorrow."

He tried to shake his head, but it hurt him to do it. "No."

"Don't you have work in the morning?"

"Work in the morning?" he said as though it were a new concept. As if he had never thought about what it meant to work in the morning. As if he didn't remember that there was anything outside of that bar.

"Come on, up." I pulled him to his feet by the arm. I was steady on my own feet, because like I said, I was in that magic alcoholic plateau where I could function normally, but clean, without the anxiety, without the bothersome thoughts that never seemed to go away, that never let me do any little piece of work or pull myself together, get a job of my own, even if it was washing dishes. It would be a comedown, but I was still a man, after all. Who was that doctor to tell me if I drank much more it would kill me? I knew what would and wouldn't kill me.

Well, I had him to his feet, like I said, and I brought him out to the curb, and he was hanging off of me completely now, and maybe I felt a little guilty, but only a little. We'd had a good time.

The bellman called a cab, and got the back door open for us. I poured Montgomery into the black plastic seat. "Where do you live?" I said.

"My notebook."

"I put it in your pocket. Tell the driver where you live." I called to the bellman, "Is there a way to put the cab on my room?"

"Certainly, sir, I'll work it out." He went around to the driver's side, and the driver rolled down his window.

Montgomery said something about Tudor Street and I felt fairly certain that he would get home all right. I said to the driver, "If you can't get him to tell you where he lives, bring him back here." He nodded, and turned back to the bellman. I closed the back door, and went back inside.

But then that empty hotel room began to loom up again. And there was a twinge, and only a twinge thanks to the alcohol, of the panic about the telegrams and Vee leaving me here. But that was silly, I told myself. Someone had recognized me, and worshipped me. If this kid reporter could, then why couldn't Joseph? But the answer was easy. He could. He just needed a chance to calm down. That was all. And he'd had a chance. All those hours, all afternoon. And it wasn't too late. Eight o'clock was early for a kid his age. That was just the start of the evening.

I turned around and went back out the revolving door. "Cab," I said, and the doorman whistled. He opened the door for me like he'd done before, and closed it when he saw I was settled. The driver had his head cocked, waiting for directions. I gave him Quinn's address—Joseph's address—and we pulled out of the circular drive onto Chase Street.

5.

The old Hadley mansion was in the neighborhood of Underwood, in the northern part of the city, just above the university. The whole area had been owned by one family up until about sixty or seventy years ago, and when they started to parcel it off and open it to development, the Hadleys took their umbrella fortune and built a four-story brick edifice into the side of a slight hill. There were pitched awnings over all the windows that made the place look like a hotel. A steep multi-tiered set of stairs rose from the street to the main entrance, while the garage and the servants' entrance was at street level in the back.

Half the lights in the house were on when the cab pulled up front. I got out and paused for a moment with the cab door still open. I turned to ask the driver to wait, but in the end I closed the door and the cabbie pulled off before I had stepped away from the curb. I started up the steep stairs, which proved to be more difficult than I expected. I mean I had had a few drinks, but it had been over a lot of hours, so there was no reason for it but I leaned a lot of my weight on the iron pipe of a railing.

Just when I was at the next-to-last landing, the front door opened, and out came Mary O'Brien and behind her Connie, both of them with their heads down, looking for the first step. I wanted to go up to meet them, but I had had enough, so I waited for them to come down. Mary saw me first, from about halfway down the top set of stairs. She caught herself up, and said, "Oh."

Connie looked up, but the light was too poor to see her expression, her black features like a shadowed mask.

Mary started down again. "Mr. Rosenkrantz, you gave me such a start." She picked her way down to the landing. "What are you doing here so late?"

I could have asked the same of her, but she was his fiancée, and she had Connie with her, no doubt as a chaperone, and hadn't it been such a tough day and all, with the will being read, and Joe becoming a millionaire. He must have needed the company to bolster his strength. "Thought I'd see Joe. Didn't realize it had gotten so late."

Her face took on a pinched look. She probably smelled the alcohol, but I tell you, I really was fine, only I guess she didn't know that. "I'm glad you're here," she said. "I was very much hoping to get a chance to talk to you."

"Well, here I am." I nodded to Connie, who said, "Mr. Rosenkrantz," and I said, "Shem, please."

"Joe was very upset," Mary said. "I mean at the—earlier. Before. He didn't…oh, you do know what I'm trying to say, don't you?"

"Yeah. Sure. It's awfully nice of you to say even if it isn't true."

"Oh, but it is. I mean, well, ask Connie. That's the only reason we're here so late. This has all been so hard on Joe. He needed me—us, somebody with him, I almost don't like to leave him now. Miss Quinn was really all he had," and realizing what she'd said, "I mean…of course he had you too—"

"And you, and Aunt Alice, and Connie here, right Connie? And any number of other people, but sure, yeah, I know what you mean. Quinn was his mom, of course he's upset. I'm here to take over for you guys. It's my shift." And I tried that dapper grin of mine, but it was probably sloppy, I was feeling a little green.

"Oh, but, I don't think now is the right time. I mean…"

"Mary," I said, "Can I call you Mary? You're doing a lot of oh-but-ing and I-mean-ing. Take a breath and just relax. If Joe's not up to my visit tonight, for any reason, sure, that's okay. I'm disappointed, but it's okay. Right?"

She took a deep breath, and when she let it out her face looked lighter. It really did. "Joe said you were so unreasonable, and really…" She turned and looked at Connie. "Connie, could you go down. I'll be right there."

"Yes, ma'am," Connie said, and stepped around her, but to me she hazarded a look and said, "Miss Alice was quite disappointed you didn't make it to tea."

"Well, Aunt Alice can add it to the list of ways I've disappointed her," I said.

Connie cringed, and really I didn't have to be so tough with her. She was just doing her job. Sometimes it was hard to remember that, it was so much like she was a member of the family, even if she was a Negro. And how awkward must that be for her, family yet not family, employee and confidante?

"Listen, Connie, I'm sorry, but you know—" I started, but the light in the front room went out just then, and we were plunged into a deeper darkness. I looked up at the windows to see if Joseph was standing there watching us. I couldn't tell, but I figured he probably was. We all paused while our eyes got used to the dark.

Then Connie said, "I'll be sure to send her your regards, Mr. Rosenkrantz." She started down the steps, leaning even more heavily on the railing than I had, dropping one foot onto the step below her, and then limping the rest of her weight after it.

Mary and I watched her for a moment, and when she was nearly to the next landing, Mary turned to me. "Mr. Rosenkrantz…" I had to resist making the wisecrack, 'Call me Dad,' but she was trying so hard, it wouldn't have been fair to her. "I know you and Joseph have had a hard time in the past."

"A hard time's hardly saying it. Last time we saw each other he took a swing at me, and that was his high school graduation."

"Yes. Oh." He hadn't told her that one.

"Look, Mary, I appreciate what you're trying to say. It was stupid of me to come up here. I've been sober for months up until today."

She gave a start at that.

"I guess this whole thing with Quinn is getting to all of us, and I…" I felt like I was maybe going to cry. I didn't, you understand, but I felt like I *might*.

She nearly put her hand out to comfort me, but thought better of it. "Maybe we can meet tomorrow," she said. "I meant to call on you at your hotel earlier, but somehow the day has slipped past. I've never been here this late, and if Connie weren't with me, my parents would have had the police out. They probably have anyway. You're... we're all tired. Can I call on you tomorrow?"

"Of course."

"I just think it would be best if we spoke tomorrow. Things aren't so simple."

"Of course, of course. A pretty girl like you? You can call on me anytime you want."

She looked down and I knew I'd spoiled it with that comment about her being pretty. She was trying, but she'd no doubt heard all of Joe's stories about my sleeping around—never mind that Quinn did too—and here I sound like I'm trying to pick her up. "Any time after breakfast, let's say. At the hotel. We can get a cup of coffee in the hotel café."

I was starting to sweat heavily then. The cloying heat and alcohol were getting to me and I felt as though I were going to be sick. It didn't help knowing Joe might be up there watching me talk to her.

"Yes, I'd like that," she said, and ventured a look at me, and then she sighed in relief and even smiled, and pretty wasn't really strong enough for what she was. Like I'd said before, Joe was a lucky man.

"After you," I said, and held my hand out to the steps in invitation. She went down before me, and I looked back up at the looming house again, but it was still impossible to know if Joe was at one of those windows. All of the other lights in the house were still on.

At the bottom of the steps, I was breathing heavily and the sweat was making me irritable, so I just said, "Ladies," and turned south on foot before they could offer me a ride or inquire after my health. Wouldn't that have been rich?

I made it to the end of the block, and I turned in, and was immediately sick on the foot of a tree. The heaves were strong enough to make my sides sore. Tears pushed out of my closed eyes. I pressed my forehead against the bark of the tree, both hands bracing me on either side, but it was only later that I felt the pain of the sharp bark cutting into me. I heaved again and the taste of alcohol and acid burned the back of my nose, and I felt chill even as the sweat poured off of me. I heaved and I heaved. A part of me marveled at the volume, but soon there was nothing coming up, and the sour smell of my vomit was sickening in its own right. I brought my forearm up, and leaned my head against that on the tree. The sweat soaked into my sleeve. I was lightheaded and I shivered as a pang went down my sides. I shivered again. And then I seemed to be finished. There was the taste in my mouth, but nothing was rebelling any longer.

I pushed myself up, and wiped my mouth with my handkerchief. Great job, I thought. A really classy guy. What would Montgomery think if he saw me now? It's not enough I owe money all over the country and depend on the whims of a hardboiled whore, I've got to drink myself sick a block from Joe's house when I've got the crazy idea about making it up. Yeah, I was nothing but a poor bastard, like I said before, and I deserved everything I got, but don't let me catch you saying it.

Once I felt sure on my feet, I stepped into the near-black street, crossing to the other side. There, a recessed footlight in a brick retaining wall revealed the vomit on the toes of my shoes. I stopped, pulled out my already soiled handkerchief and, leaning against the wall, lifted one foot, wiped it off, and then the other. When I was done, I threw the handkerchief into the gutter, and started south towards the less residential part of the city near the university where I'd be able to find a cab.

The lights came first, and then the lawns ended, and there was a five-story apartment house visible across University Avenue. If I looked straight down St. Peter's Street, I could see the lights of the skyscrapers all the way downtown. The roads were empty, and the traffic light went through its pattern needlessly as, still shaky, I crossed University into George Village. Quinn and I used to hang around George Village to be with people our own age, and she knew some men at the university. Not much had changed in the intervening years. The row homes hidden by overgrown trees looked broken down and abused, which they were, rented short-term to college men who took the job of being college men very seriously.

When I got to the block where the George Village Pub was, I still hadn't run into a cab. I was starting to feel a bit hungry, my stomach now empty after my little spell. I pushed into the stale smoke of the bar, and was comforted to find that I didn't look too out of place. The students were away for the summer, so the only people in the bar that night were some loud and coarse citybillies and a few grad students trying to keep their heads down. I ordered a Gin Rickey. The bartender sighed and took his time getting to the hard stuff. In a place like that the only kind of orders they get are draught and the bartender gets lazy. But he made me the drink.

With the first swallow, I felt calmer. I pushed the whole pathetic incident, the talk with Mary, the puking, pushed it all away, and my mind turned to the play Montgomery and I had been working on that evening. And just like the old days, the thought of having to write more tomorrow clenched my heart in a vise. I didn't want to; I couldn't; the burn of vomit in the back of my throat made my stomach turn; I'd just tell Montgomery to forget it, I was too busy.

Then all of a sudden, something clicked: the Furies in our little play could die, be killed themselves, that is. The vise relaxed, and I took another drink. It's like that sometimes. An idea at the end of the night hits, and you feel, at least I've got somewhere to start tomorrow. Well, I felt good about that idea, less anxious about the next day, and after two more drinks, I started to think about visiting Joe again. The idea of my hotel room didn't strike me as any more appealing now. If he threw me out or took a swing at me, it'd still be better than the hotel.

I thought about another drink, patted my pockets for a little cash, but of course I didn't have any, so I went out back where the bathrooms were. I pushed my way through a door marked "Exit," and found myself in the alley behind the bar. I ran as fast as my aching body would let me back up to the next block, and when I came out in the street, I walked one block east to Caroline Street in order to make my way back to University.

6.

Nothing had changed in the hour since I'd been turned away. The little sprint from the bar had me sweating worse than before, and I was angry, no, irritable, eager to get in where it was air-conditioned at least. I pressed on the buzzer when I got to the top of the stairs and took off my jacket. I mopped my forehead, my face, the back of my neck with the sleeves of my shirt. The whole idea of being there in the middle of the night struck me as crazy again. How could I expect that he would open the door? I mean, I probably could have walked right in, they never used to lock their doors in that neighborhood, but that wouldn't do. I pressed the buzzer again, figuring just the last time, and the door swung open immediately. He must have been standing right on the other side.

"What do you want?" he said. He was still dressed, but his collar was unbuttoned and he wasn't wearing a tie.

"Joe, I—" I hadn't thought of what I was going to say to him if he did answer. "Can I come in?"

"What do you want?"

"Can't I just come in?"

"What do you want?" He was sneering, but he hadn't closed the door.

"To talk," I spat out. "To talk. Come on, Joe, we should be friends. We should…now, you know—if we're all that's left… Can't I just come in?"

He took a step back, and I thought he was going to slam the door, I really did. And oh, if he had... Well I wouldn't be where I am now, would I? But he took a step back and said, "Do what you want." And walked away from the door, leaving it open.

I stepped inside and closed the door behind me. I hadn't been in that house since I don't know when. They'd pulled up the Persian rug that used to be in the front hall, revealing the black-and-white chessboard tiles. The grandfather clock was also gone, replaced by a wall-mounted brass starburst with no digits and a long pendulum. Joe had gone into the further room to the right, the dining room, where he stood at a glass-topped brass refreshment cart. He was pouring a brandy. There was a glass on the dining room table with melting ice and an amber residue in it already, so at first I thought he was making me a drink, but he brought the glass to his own lips. It was then that it hit me he was drunk too, drunker even than I was.

"Joe, what can I do to make it up with you?" I said, the table between us.

"You can't."

"Well can you at least tell me what it is I'm supposed to have done? How can I try to explain myself, if I don't even know what it is I have to explain?"

"You don't have to explain yourself. I know already. I was here, remember? I was the one who had to watch Mom suffer. You were off with, who is it now? Are you and Chloë still married even? I can't remember. Not that it would matter to you."

"You just wait until you're married," I said, angry now

myself. Somehow the air conditioner wasn't doing its job. "You don't know."

"I know I would never do to Mary what you did to Mom."

"You think I planned it? I didn't plan it."

"But you did it."

"Come on. What is this? You're twenty-one—"

"Twenty-two."

I wished I hadn't gotten that wrong. But I went on, "Right, twenty-two. You're just a kid. You'll learn that when you're older—"

"I am older." His glass shook in his hands. "I'm not a kid anymore."

"No, you're not a kid. I don't mean to say you're a kid. I mean things just look different when…" I took a breath. "You know I wasn't the only one being unfaithful. Your mother was there right along with me."

His lips were quaking despite his efforts to maintain control. "You would speak on the dead."

I lost it for a moment then. "Listen, you— Just shut up and listen. All of this, this crap you're on about, it all happened before you were born, so what do you know about it anyway? You weren't there!"

He raised his voice too. "And you weren't here for the last twenty-two years, so what do you know about it! Mom was…she never…she was…you had Chloë Rose, not that she was enough for you either, but Mom just had, she only had…" He brought the glass to his lips and it was shaking.

I steadied myself on the back of one of the chairs. "Joe, what's this really all about? This is all ancient history.

Let's forget all of that. I'm here now to try and make it different."

He took another drink from his glass. The ice clinked. There was nothing left in the glass to drink.

"You know, I met a guy today, about your age. And he, well, he just about thinks I'm the greatest thing on two legs, and I thought, why couldn't my boy feel that way? Why couldn't Joe feel that way? And I thought, sure he could. There's no reason he couldn't."

He took another drink from his empty glass, his lip still trembling and his hand unsteady.

"I'm not all bad," I said.

"What you did to Mom—"

"Oh stop it," I spat. "You don't know a damn thing about it. You don't know how often she'd be out and I'd be in one hotel or another all by myself, or even worse, when she would come back to the room with someone and it didn't even matter I was there. Don't go on about how Quinn was some kind of martyr. She kept me on the hook for alimony and child support the whole time too, even though I couldn't pay it and she didn't need it. She wanted me to know she could send me to jail any time she wanted."

"Of course it's about the money with you. That's why you're really here."

"Damn it, Joe. You say you're grown up, but you're acting like a brat."

"Tell me you don't want the money. Tell me that you weren't drinking yourself dumb today after you got nothing in that will."

"Forget the damn money. This isn't about the money.

What do I have to say to prove it to you? Your mother cared more about the money than I ever did."

"Mom suffered. She, you don't know…she wasted away. Her body, it just, it fell off her somehow. She lost a lot of her hair." There were tears falling down his cheeks, but he hadn't given in to them. He wasn't all-out crying just yet. He swallowed and shut it down. "I had to face that alone, just like always. I had to help her to the bathroom. I had to sit in the hospital waiting for it. It was me. And her life was just, it, she wasn't, it could have been so much more. I could have done more." This last line came out in a squeak, and he shook his head.

"Joe…"

He shook his head more, and he turned and walked through the swinging door back to the kitchen. He'd been all over the place, I had cheated on Quinn, I wanted her money, I didn't know what her death was like. It didn't matter what I said, he was poisoned against me, and in his eyes, there was nothing I could do right. But still I followed him.

He was at the sink with his back to me, but I could tell he was crying. "Joe?"

No response.

"I loved your mother. I—"

He spun around and flung the glass at me. It went wide and hit the wall, spraying melted ice water in a splatter along the paint. The glass broke neatly in two.

We both waited, shocked by the violence. Joe cried and fought crying at the same time, which only contorted his face worse than if he'd let go. I tried to count to ten, which I'd never done before, but I was with a girl for a little while who did it all the time and swore it worked. I couldn't make it all the way to ten, but when I spoke, I felt steady and I didn't yell.

"I loved Quinn very much, more than anyone except for Clotilde maybe. I can't even believe that she's dead. She was out there for so long..."

"Like you," Joe said, not able to fight the crying anymore. Standing there with his fists clenched, crying openly, well it was enough to bring tears to my eyes too, and that meant I loved him too, right? I mean, of course it did. "When I was a kid, I worshipped you," Joe said, his voice erratic as he sobbed. "You meet some kid in a bar and you feel important because he looks up to you. As a writer. I worshipped you for being my father."

I waited. Let him get it out.

"It was hard living with Mom. And Grandma and Grandpa. Knowing you were out there, though, that you were famous..." The crying renewed itself. "And those times I flew out to California, and you couldn't be bothered with me, and you were loud and drunk and you fought with Chloë, with everybody. What do you think that did to me?"

I just shook my head.

"Even after the first time and after the second time, it got harder and harder. It took me a while, but I figured it out, that I meant nothing to you and you weren't so great, in fact, you were pretty terrible."

"I'm sorry."

"That doesn't mean anything."

I stepped forward, reaching out for him. "I'm sorry. I was, when I was drinking, horrible."

He snuffed at that. "*When* you were drinking?"

"You can ask anybody, I've been sober for months. This…well, like I said, I loved Quinn, and I don't have to tell you." I nodded at him.

"No. Because I don't care."

"You're the one who's crying."

"You betrayed me."

"By being different than something you made up in your head?" I said, my voice rising again.

"By everything!" He started forward, but he had to pass me to get to the door. I reached out to stop him, and he jerked away, and lashed out with his arm, striking mine away, but I managed to stay between him and the door. "Stop it! Let me go!"

"Joe, I'm your father," I said, reaching out for his shoulder again.

"No!" He fought me, and our arms got tangled, and he landed a few accidental blows and I'm sure I did the same, and then he pushed me away and turned to the refrigerator and pulled from beside it an ice pick and then swept around at me, brandishing the ice pick as a deterrent only I'm sure.

I pulled back. "What are you doing?"

"Get out," he said, panting. His eyes were red from crying, but he wasn't crying anymore. His face was pure malice.

"You're not going to—" I said, walking towards him again. And don't ask me what I was going to do. I was going to hug him, I guess, even though it sounds kind of sappy. But when you spend too long in Hollywood, what do you expect? You turn sappy. So I took a step towards him, and he lunged.

The ice pick struck me a glancing blow, tearing my shirt, a hot flash crossed my bicep. And I guess I threw my arms up, or pushed, or something, we were so close together at that point, and I think I was probably just trying to knock the ice pick out of his hands, but instead, he tripped and he fell backwards and there was a clunk, like the sound of a grapefruit dropping, as the back of his head hit the edge of the counter, and his chin raced against his chest and he fell to the floor in a heap.

I had my right hand over the cut in my left arm, the pain like a paper cut multiplied by a thousand if you can imagine that. And there was blood dripping down my sleeve from between my fingers, and I know from later that some of it dripped on the floor.

Joe was unconscious. That's what I thought. But I probably knew.

"Joe," I said.

He didn't say anything.

"Joe? Are you all right?"

I kicked his foot, lightly, to try to wake him, but it just jostled his leg, and he didn't move. Fear started racing up my arms and into my jaw. I bent down. The back of his head didn't look too bad, what I could see of it, although the hair was matted from the blood, and his head was at a funny angle. "Joe?"

I didn't try to touch him, because by then I knew. Maybe it was the bump on his head or maybe he had broken his neck. The ice pick was on the floor only a few inches from his hand, the end spotted with blood. I was shivering all over, still gripping my cut arm, and if I hadn't vomited so much before, I would have vomited then, my throat constricted, my mouth dry.

I wanted to cry, but instead my heart was racing.

I don't know how long I crouched there. My thighs started to burn. But it was the sound of the telephone ringing that jarred me out of my stupor.

I stood up, and I don't know why I did it, except maybe that a phone rings and you answer, so I answered.

7.

"Joe? Are you still awake?" It was a whisper.

"Who is this?" I said.

The voice on the other end got tight and a touch louder. "Who is this?"

It was Mary. How could I talk to Mary now? "Joe just went out to the bathroom, and then I'm going to get him in bed, I promise," I said, it just coming out natural like that.

"Mr. Rosenkrantz?"

"I got to thinking I should give Joe a try anyway, and I'm glad I did, because we had a swell time. I'm just about leaving. Should I have Joe call you when he gets out of the bathroom?"

"No, no, it's late," she said. And lucky for me she did. What would I have done if she'd said yes? "I'm glad you're there. I was really worried. He shouldn't be alone."

"He's feeling better now."

"Good. Very good. I'm so glad things worked out." She did sound glad about it, relieved almost. "We still have our date for the morning though?"

"I wouldn't miss it," I said, and I was even grinning my patented grin, even if my throat was dry. You can hear someone smile over the telephone.

"Good night."

"Good night," I said and hung up.

Then I was alone with my son again. Alone with his corpse. I had killed my son. I didn't mean it. Nobody could say I meant it. He had attacked me. The blood was trickling down my arm. My son was dead. I needed to go. I needed help. If I were writing a movie, what would I have the murderer do? I didn't know. I never got the hang of those murder stories. That's why nobody in Hollywood would hire me.

All this time I was trying to look everywhere but at his body, but then I saw him again, and the lump in my throat was a baseball that was choking me. Vee would know what to do. Vee was...

I needed a drink. I needed to get out of there. That was definitely what I needed to do. As soon as the thought occurred to me, I went into action. I went back through the swinging doors, through the dining room, grabbing my coat, over the chessboard floor and out into the night. I took the stairs two at a time.

The heat was oppressive. But I was nearly running, and I went like that the whole mile and a half or so back to George Village. The pain in my arm had dulled, maybe from the exertion, but I could see from the streetlights that it was still bleeding. I stopped to put on my coat. It was like a razor searing my arm as I slid the coat sleeve over the cut and twisted to get the other arm in. The renewed pain throbbed before settling back to a dull ache. Then, luck would have it, a car turned onto University from Caroline, heading towards me as I crossed University at St. Peter's. The headlights resolved themselves, and I saw it was a cab. I flagged it down, and ran up to it even as it was coming to a stop in the southbound lane on St. Peter's. The cabbie was a rare man—a driver who didn't try to talk your ear off, so I didn't have to try at small talk I was in no state to conduct. With no traffic, it took only ten minutes to get back to the hotel.

Then I was in the room. The window air conditioners had been on full blast, and the place felt like a refrigerator. It made the hairs on my arms stand up, and sent a shiver across my shoulders, which shot pain through my arm. I slipped out of my jacket, pulling the right sleeve off first and then gingerly sliding the coat off my left arm. The bleeding had stopped. My shirtsleeve was stuck to me with dried blood, and I pulled it free, a satisfying little tug, and tried to see the cut. It wasn't anything serious, not much more than a scratch, and I guess that was something to be happy about. Yeah, thank God for the small things, never mind the—well, just never mind...

I checked my jacket. The blood hadn't soaked through. I turned the sleeve inside out. There was a slight black smudge there, but that was all right. I righted the sleeve and tossed the jacket at the couch, missed, and left it there.

I kept standing there in the center of the living room with that whooshing hiss of the air conditioners deafening me as I tried to make sense of the suite. The maid had made up the bed and vacuumed the carpet and the place was so clean it was antiseptic, with that unreal sense of domesticity that hotels have, the furniture set up like someone were living here but without any of the telltale signs—a lamp off center on a side table, stubs and ashes in the ashtrays, a book laid out, hell, any books at all.

And, of course, Vee wasn't there.

The sweat had dried on me, a salty skin that made me feel unclean. I started nodding my head, just nodding. At what I do not know, but nodding all the same. Joe was gone. I had killed him. I had killed a man. I was going to go to prison. Did they have the death penalty in Maryland? I couldn't remember. I thought they did. I was going to go to the electric chair. Or maybe it was the gas chamber. And Joe was dead. I had killed him. I had killed a man? I was going to go to prison. And around and around like that for who knows how long, but you get the idea.

Then I thought I should really get some sleep. I had a meeting with Joe's fiancée in the morning, and I was supposed to see the Montgomery kid too. I needed to be rested. And I know it was crazy to be thinking about things like I'd be able to keep my appointments, but *you* kill a man and tell me you don't think crazy things. I started unbuttoning my shirt, but I hadn't made it two buttons when the image of Joe lying there in the kitchen came back to me strong and I rushed for the bathroom, because this time I thought I would throw up again. But when I was on the floor in the bathroom with the cold porcelain in my hands, I only gave one belch that was half cough, and then just stayed there with my head hanging down near the toilet water and the cold of the tile floor bleeding in through my pants.

The cold woke me up again. I couldn't go to prison. Who would look after Clotilde? I had been living in the YMCA so that the last of her movie money could go to keeping her in the hospital, but the money was running out, and I couldn't let Clotilde go to a state hospital; they butchered the patients at those places, all of them walking around like empty spirits, drool hanging from their lips, a bunch of drug addicts and maniacs. That was why I was out here in the first place, grasping at straws, because while Vee had rescued me from the Y as a charity case, I needed to come up with Clotilde's hospital money myself, and I couldn't do it in prison. I had to do something. I had to—I didn't know. I couldn't think of anything, not one thing.

But Vee would probably know. Vee's friend Carlton would definitely know. He was a gangster, wasn't he?

I reached my hand into my pants pocket and clutched the hotel key with its plastic diamond tag that read "Suite 12-2." They were sure to be able to help me. I didn't need to go to prison. Nobody needed to know at all. It could have been an accident. It was an accident. I just needed somebody to show me how to...how to make it all okay.

I was up and moving then. I went out in the hallway, forgetting that I was wearing a torn and bloody shirt, that was how out of it I was, and I went to the stairwell because it was closer than the elevators, and so I had to climb I can't tell you how many steps, but it was a lot of steps. The stairwell wasn't air conditioned, of course, and the sweat was pouring off of me. I kept taking breaks at the landings, checking the cut to make sure it hadn't started bleeding again. Finally at the twelfth floor, I pulled open the door. My heart was pounding, and I was out of breath, and I was overheated and dripping, and it all put me in more of a panic.

There were only four suites on the twelfth floor. These

were the luxury suites. The grand suites. Vee had said
that Carlton kept Suite 12-2 in perpetuity even though
he had a house uptown and one on the Eastern Shore
and spent maybe three weeks worth of nights at the hotel
in a year, if that.

The door to Suite 12-2 was twenty feet from the stairwell with maybe another fifteen feet between the door and
the elevators. It was very quiet. The eternally burning
hall lights felt defiant so late at night, almost as though
they were saying they didn't need people, they could do
fine on their own, thank you. See, I told you I was screwy.

I stood in front of the suite door. My heart was
pounding, my arm was aching, I swallowed but my throat
was dry. I raised my hand to knock, but managed nothing
more than a tap, so of course there wasn't any response.
My nerves grew shakier. I couldn't bring myself to knock
again, and I couldn't keep standing there in the hallway
with a bloody shirt and a glistening brow. So I took the
key, which was still in my hand, slid it into the lock, and
opened the door.

8.

There was a light on. I could see that before I had the door open enough to see anything else. There was a galley kitchen immediately to the left of the door that ran for several feet, and there was a bank of mirrored sliding closet doors to the right. The light I had seen was a reflection in the mirror; the entryway was actually quite shadowed.

I stepped past the kitchen into a big open space with a dining room table to the left and living room furniture a little further on. The furniture was organized around a glass coffee table, taking full advantage of the large windows that offered a wide view of the city. In the far corner there was an armchair lit by a standing lamp, and in the chair, a book closed over one finger on his lap, was an enormous man—it was hard to say just how big with him sitting. He wore a pair of blue-and-white striped pajamas with a mauve silk robe over it and a pair of leather slippers. He looked at me with open amazement.

"Who—the hell—are you?" he said, almost biting off each word, his amazement turning fast to anger.

"I'm sorry, I—"

He raised his bulk and he was big like a gorilla. "Who the hell are you." He let the book fall to the floor, and it lay open in the middle.

"I just…Mr. Carlton."

"Mr. Carlton? Mr. Carlton?" He was advancing on me.

I thought I was going to cry. I really did. How would that have been, me crying in front of a gangster? "Those who address me," he was yelling, "address me as Mr. Browne, but that's just those who address me." There was still half the room between us. He was livid, but he wasn't too concerned about getting at me. "You better talk or you won't be able to talk no more."

Vee appeared from the hallway at the left in a short robe. "Shem!" she said. "Carlton... I mean Mr. Rosenkrantz, what's going on?"

Carlton; Mr. Browne—how was I supposed to know Carlton was his first name?—Mr. Browne yelled without turning around, "You know this man, Victoria?"

"No," she said, looking at me with complete shock. "I mean, yeah. He's my cousin."

"What's your 'cousin' doing in my suite at nearly two in the goddamn morning?"

She started across the room then. She had her face in a pretty good imitation of honest confusion. "I saw him this afternoon. I lost my key. Shem, you should have just left it at the front desk with a note."

He grabbed her by the arm and pulled her around.

"Oh, Carlton!"

He must have squeezed tighter, because she winced.

"Carlton...please."

"This is your cousin? How old is he?"

"Oh, I don't know." She was struggling to keep her face composed. "Shem...?"

I held the key out, like that was going to make it better. This was a man who wanted his girlfriends to carry guns and was just about breaking Vee's arm. "I'm sorry," I said, and I *sounded* like I was going to cry. "It's just that I killed him, and I didn't know what to do."

He took a step towards me, pulling Vee with him. She was looking at me with terror, trying to shake her head so that I'd see but he wouldn't.

"Excuse me," he said.

"He's dead," I said, still holding out the key.

"Carlton, please…" Vee said. He threw her to the side and she tripped but caught herself against the wall so she didn't go down.

"I'll tell you what," he said, and he was smiling as he said it, which was much worse than when he was angry. "I don't feel much like ruining this robe, and I just had a manicure this morning, so I'm going to go back in my room for my baseball bat, and if you're still here when I get back, I'll show you what to do when you kill somebody."

Vee took a step towards him, "Carlton—"

He punched her in the face and her head swung around and she fell into a dining room chair and then sat on the ground. "That goes for you too," he said to her, walking away from us.

Vee looked up at me from the ground. There was a large red blotch on the left side of her face that was already becoming puffy. "You bastard," she said, and started to try and pull herself up with the help of the chair she had fallen into.

"Vee, I didn't know what else to do. I killed Joseph, and—"

"Stop saying that!" She grabbed onto me to steady herself. "Come on, or are you really that stupid?"

"You're not wearing any—"

She pushed me back towards the hall door, got it opened, and went right for the stairs, dragging me along. "I could kill you. I should kill you."

We were in the hot stairwell. The room key was still in my hand, and I slipped it back into my pocket as Vee started down ahead of me. "I told you I was only joking," she yelled back up at me, her voice echoing. "You weren't supposed to go and do it."

And it hit me that she had told me to kill him this afternoon. And had that been in the back of my mind when I went to see him? Had I killed him because I actually wanted to? The money would be mine now—he wasn't married yet, he had no will, I was his closest living relative. I realized just how much trouble I was in, because nobody would believe it was an accident now, even if I tried to say it was. I had too good a motive. But I hadn't meant to kill him. It had been an accident.

Vee was a whole level below me. She pushed out onto our floor, and the door had already closed behind her when I got to it, but she had to wait at our room, because I had the key. She had her arms crossed just under her breasts as though she was cold, but really she had caught an unnatural case of modesty. She shoved me aside once the door was unlocked and was at the armoire already by the time I made it into the bedroom. She took out a skirt and a blouse and flung them on the bed.

"You're really crazy, you know that? He could have killed us both. He probably will kill me. What am I to him? I'm just another whore." She was getting dressed, not taking the time to hide her nakedness now. "He's not so foolish to think I'm with him alone, but to have another man show up in his room. Like Samson and Delilah." She had the skirt on now, and was zipping it up. Then she pulled it around so the zipper was in the back. "We need to get out of here."

"Vee," I said, and I don't know what was in my voice, but she stopped and looked at me.

"What the hell happened to your arm?"

"Joe stabbed me with an ice pick."

She got very calm. "You're serious? You really killed him?"

I just nodded. I couldn't talk then.

"S—t! S—t, s—t, s—t."

"It was an accident."

"Who saw you?"

I shook my head. "When?"

"When! When! Now, you idiot. Who saw you? Who'd you tell? What happened?" She started putting her blouse on, but her fingers were shaking so much as she tried to work the buttons that it took several attempts with each one.

"I don't think anybody saw me. It was at his house. It was an accident."

"Like anyone will believe that."

"It was!"

"All right! Don't yell at me about it. I believe you it was an accident. But who else will believe you!" She had her shirt mostly buttoned. Her face was bruising.

"I ran out. It was dark. I took a cab here, and I don't know. I guess I came through the lobby."

She gestured at my bloody arm with her head. "With that?"

"I had my jacket on."

She paused. "Can we get back in the house? Is it locked?"

"I don't know. I don't think so. Probably not. It never used to be."

She went past me, finishing the last button and picked up the phone. "Yes, could you have Mr. Browne's car around front please?" She paused. "Thank you, I'll be right down."

"What are you doing?" I said.

She picked up my jacket and pushed it at me, pushing me towards the door at the same time. "You go down the stairs and out through the back. Make sure no one sees you. Wait around the corner and I'll be there to get you."

"What are you going to do?"

"Fix it. That's what you wanted, didn't you?"

"Vee, are you okay?"

Her face was purple and black, her eye had red in it. She looked like she was going to claw me. But instead, before I could say anything more, she was off to the elevators, striding away from me with all the assurance in the world.

I felt exhausted all of a sudden, and slumped against the wall. How could I get up? How could I ever walk again? My eyes closed and my head sagged. Quinn, I thought. Clotilde... Again the sight of Joe's head flopped over on his neck came before me, and it made my stomach turn. But it got me going. I went back to the stairs, and went down, down in the fiery heat.

9.

Vee was angry. She kept her jaw set and her eyes on the road. We only spoke enough for me to give her directions. The city was asleep and we had the road to ourselves. "Are we close?" Vee said up around the train station where a handful of cabs sat out front waiting for a late train to come in.

"About halfway," I said.

"Let me know when we're close. We can't park nearby."

She was like that, all business, and I got the feeling that she wasn't angry that I had killed Joe, not the killing itself so much, but angry at the annoyance of it. And of course she was really angry that I had gotten her in dutch with Carlton. Browne. Whatever his name was.

At the university I told her we were nearby and she pulled off on 34th Street, went over to Caroline, and turned the car back south. She found a spot about midway up the block. We got out and she came around the car. "Take my arm," she said. "We're just coming home from a night on the town."

I led the way and the sweat was pouring off of me again. It had been a relief of sorts when Vee took over—that *is* what I had wanted—but now the idea of having to go back into that house again, of having to see him again,

I wasn't sure if I could do it. Things could be that way, a place you went to every day, so often you didn't even see it anymore, you knew every inch of it so well, a place like that and a little time goes by, or something happens… well sometimes a place that was like home could suddenly feel like the strangest place in the world. And I started to feel that way as we were walking in the dark, in the shadows of the trees along the road with the lights out in all of the houses and not a single car on the street. It started to seem like I'd never been in Underwood before, hell, like I'd never been to Calvert City before.

But I had been. I'd been there nearly every day for over a year and more besides when I was courting Quinn and then after we were married. And it wasn't the time. It was the thing. I had better look at it because I'd have to look at it soon enough. It was Joe being dead. It was why Joe was dead.

I must have faltered in my step, because Vee's hand on my arm tightened to where I could feel her fingertips digging into my arm through my jacket, and she kept me moving. "Oh no you don't," she said. "You're going through with this now or you don't want to know what'll happen."

Yeah, I was going through with it, because I had already, hadn't I? I'd gone about as far through with it as you could, and it was my deal. The whole neighborhood looked foreign to me, but I knew right where I was going, and I'd better get there.

"Can we come up from behind the place? That would be better."

I didn't answer, but I took us around the block where

we would come up on the side of the house near the driveway and the servants' entrance. I didn't know that it would be open, but when we tried the door it was unlocked.

It was dark inside, but we only needed to make our way up the stairs, and then… I was more lost in the house than I had been outside. It somehow felt as though it were expanding and contracting at the same time if you can imagine that. Like the house was the whole world, so huge I couldn't ever hope to get through it in a hundred thousand lifetimes, but also so small that I was trapped inside, unable to move, the very walls crushing in on me, choking me, my throat, my shoulders, my chest, my heart, all of it pulling in. This wasn't Quinn's house. This wasn't the place where I once walked around completely naked, the time the Hadleys were off on a cruise and Quinn and I crashed on our way to New York or from New York or somewhere anyways. This wasn't the place where old man Hadley had put his arm around me in his office and told me that he didn't trust me but that his daughter was sure stuck on me and so he couldn't but give us his approval. No, this couldn't be that house, because this was the house in which Joe and I had fought. This was where I chased him and then he tried to push me or I pushed him or, somehow I got cut, and I, or Joe, yeah, this was where it happened, so it couldn't be that other place from long ago.

"Come on," Vee said, pushing me from behind. "We don't have all night. The faster we are the better. And keep away from the windows."

I started forward, although I don't remember moving, and I took her into the kitchen and nothing had changed,

he was lying there on the floor with his head bashed in
and the ice pick near his hand. I went numb. Vee ducked
down, squatting, and hissed at me, "Get down."

I did, and I didn't have any trouble after that. I was
shut off. I was a million miles away.

"You got some blood on the floor here," Vee said, on
her hands and knees. "Wipe it up." She went over to
where his body was, and that's all it was now, just a thing.
"We've got to wipe the ice pick and put that back." She
looked back at me. "Well, hurry." I must have looked confused. "Use your sleeve." I started to reach. "No, your
shirtsleeve. The one that's already got blood on it."

I took off my jacket, and I bent down to wipe up the
spot of blood. I wouldn't have even noticed it, it was so
small. It had dried so I wet my finger with spit and then
rubbed at the spot until it was gone and wiped my finger
on my shirtsleeve near the cut. Vee handed back the ice
pick and I did the same with that, wetting it and rubbing
it on my sleeve, wetting it and rubbing. It was a tedious
job and I thought, why couldn't I just use the sink. That's
really what I was thinking. Not that I was cleaning up my
blood, because I couldn't think of that, you see. But why
couldn't I use the sink. Of course, Vee was probably right
about the windows.

While I was doing that, Vee was looking around, exam-
ining everything. She tried to lean Joe forward, but the
body was already set up some, and it was heavy, so it just
sort of slid to the side. She looked at me, and I was just
watching her. "Well, are you finished? Put that back, and
come over here and wipe this counter and cabinet. We
don't want any blood down here."

Down here? Where else were we going? But I crawled over to the refrigerator and slid the ice pick back where Joe had taken it from as nearly as I could tell, and then I crawled over beside him and Vee. If a place turns all funny once you've killed a man, just try crawling around in one. It's a whole new room.

"Couldn't I use the sink?" I said, looking at the few smudges of blood.

"Just hurry." She was exasperated. And her face really looked terrible, the bruise spread now from over her eye all along the side and across the cheekbone. It must have hurt to talk. "Take a picture, why don't you? I should have come done this myself, but I wouldn't be able to carry him alone."

So I reached up to the sink, still on the floor, and wet the edge of my sleeve, and then I wiped up the blood on the edge of the counter and the front of the cabinet. There wasn't much, like I said, and I had that pretty much cleaned up, and Vee started tugging on Joe's body, getting him over on his side. The sound of his shoes scuffing on the floor was about one of the worst things I'd ever heard. Because I'd seen a body in worse shape once, although I didn't like to think of it, but the sound of the shoes, that was, well, that was sort of normal, and nothing about any of this was normal, so it kind of got to me. Maybe I was just loopy, so you can't understand, but that's the way I felt, I'm telling you.

"Turn off the light," Vee said, "and then help me with this."

I crawled over to where the light switch was, and I saw the broken glass that was still on the floor against the wall, so I went over towards that, figuring we ought to clean that up too.

"What are you doing!" Vee snapped. "I said get the light."

"But the glass—"

"Leave it. That's a good thing. See, he was drunk, right?, and upset. So he threw his glass at the wall, right? So when he passes out with a lit cigarette in his hand, it makes it look better."

"What do you mean with a cigarette?"

"Would you just turn out the light? You think the sun's going to stay down forever? How long do you think I can have Carlton's car out? Now move. Can you do that? I need you to move."

So I moved. I got the light out, and Vee stood up immediately, and went around the body. "You get him under the arms, I'll get the feet."

We tried it like that a couple of times, but it wasn't going to work. His body was in a weird position, which threw the weight off, and Vee wasn't too strong. So at last, I pulled him up as best I could and flung him over my shoulder in a fireman carry. I staggered and started to feel lightheaded immediately, but I had him up.

"Do you know which one's his room?"

"I think," I managed.

"Okay," Vee said and started out ahead of me. Only, wait, she must have picked up my jacket, yeah, because she gave it back to me upstairs. But I wasn't really seeing where we were going or even thinking much about what we were doing anymore. I was just trying to get one foot in front of the other and not drop him as I held my breath under the exertion, only able to take quick pants every few seconds or so.

Vee turned off the lights ahead of me as we went, asking, "This way? This way?" And I would just nod, and she would turn off a light, and we got to the foot of the stairs, and I said, "There's a light up front."

"Leave it," she said. "Only the ones going up to the bedroom."

The stairs were brutal. I staggered to get my foot up on the first step, and I almost dropped him and I banged into the banister, which gave a little under the weight but held. So Vee rushed back around behind me, slipping past in the tight space, and she pushed me up from behind, and that actually did the trick, taking just enough weight off of me so that I could manage one step at a time, resting for a minute against the wall at each step. Vee kept saying, "Okay? Okay?", nervous, but I needed to take a rest. I wasn't sure if I was even going to make it at all.

We got to the top of the stairs, and I almost dropped him then, but managed to say between my teeth, "I can't hold it much longer." I took a few rushed shuffling steps into the room immediately to the right at the top of the stairs and was relieved to find that it was still Joe's room. It didn't look that different from when he had me up in it as a boy once when Clotilde and I laid over in Calvert on a trip to France.

I staggered across the room, and the light went out when I was only halfway to the bed, and then I dropped him there, the bed creaking and banging against the wall at the headboard. I fell down on the bed on top of him for a moment, and it was all I could do to breathe, there were black-and-white stars before my eyes and my head felt so heavy, and there was a pain in my neck and the cut on my arm.

Vee pulled at me, trying to get to Joe. At last I was able to focus enough to realize I was lying on top of a dead body—on top of my son's dead body!—and my stomach turned over and I rolled off of him onto my back and tried to get to my feet, but had to just lie there.

Meanwhile, Vee went through his pockets. "Where does he keep his cigarettes? Help me."

I started to roll to my feet, trying to remember if Joe smoked, but she didn't need my help by then. She had the cigarettes and was looking for the matches, running her hands over his body in the dark, with just barely some light coming in from outside, or maybe my eyes had just gotten used to the dark.

She felt her way along the bedside table and then opened the top drawer, and I could hear her messing through various things, scraping the wood in the drawer, and at last the sound stopped, and there was a flicker, and her face was suddenly illuminated. It was a Zippo. The light went out. I was blinded again. She turned the pack of cigarettes over in her hand, got one out, put it in her mouth, and the flame again.

She stood there, crouched, smoking for a moment.

"What are you doing," I hissed, although there was no reason we had to worry about being quiet.

She whispered back, "It's got to be smoked down a little. You never know how much things are going to burn."

"Burn?" But I guess I sort of got what she was planning then, and it didn't seem too crazy. It seemed like it just might work. Because why couldn't I have left, and then a couple hours later, Joe throws a glass against the wall, goes upstairs, turns off the lights as he goes—he's drunk so he leaves lights on in the other rooms—manages to light a cigarette and then pass out, and then the bed catches fire. You hear about that all the time, why they're always saying you shouldn't smoke in bed, and every time you do it, you think, that's never going to happen to me.

Vee put the cigarette near Joe's hand, still burning. Then to make sure, she took the Zippo, and held it to the comforter near the cigarette, waiting for it to catch. It flared up almost immediately, and then died down a little, and we stood there watching it, the orange glow of the flames lighting the room immediately and then growing, and soon there was some heat you could feel too.

Vee wiped the Zippo against the bed on all sides and then holding it by her fingernails, she tossed it at the bedside table where it struck and fell on the floor. That seemed to satisfy her. She turned. "Come on."

But I stayed still, watching. I hadn't really known this man. I'd known him as a boy, or at least had an idea of him then when I'd see him every few months. Okay, at least once a year. But he had been right. I didn't know him. And so, in some ways, it was like being at a funeral for a stranger. You felt crummy, but you didn't really care all that much. No, that's not true, because I cared way the hell too much. I cared so much that I didn't care.

The flames had really spread, and there was smoke in the air. Vee yelled, "Shem! Come on. Now!"

She grabbed at my shoulder, and I let her pull me away. We went back the way we had come, down the stairs, down the back stairs to the servants' entrance, out into the hot night, and back around the corner, and Vee had her arm looped in mine, and was setting a leisurely pace.

"You don't have to worry," she said, and she sounded relieved herself. "It'll be fine now." I didn't say anything. And then she hit my arm, a slight slap. "You goddamn bastard. You rich goddamn bastard. Two million dollars!"

And I was confused. What two million dollars?

"I could kill you though. Ooo, my face hurts something fierce, you goddamn bastard pimp. Carlton could have killed me." She slapped me again. "He could have killed us both. And he doesn't need to burn a house down to get rid of a couple of bodies, let me tell you." She was almost laughing now, she was so relieved. "Two million dollars! I knew there was a reason I got mixed up with you. I'd started to wonder, but I knew. I'm a smart one. I always know."

We were across University in George Village. A streetlight must have caught us, because I could feel that she was looking at me, and once we were in the shadow of a tree, she pulled around so she was standing in front of me.

"Oh, baby," she said, and she reached up and brushed my face and I could feel that it was wet. "Oh, my poor, poor baby."

"What…"

But she pulled me in to her, and pulled my head to her shoulder. She put her hand on the back of my head and ran her fingers in my hair and held me, and it felt good, because my shoulders were shaking, and my face was wet, because, I'm not afraid to say it, I was crying.

10

In the morning I woke up in the hotel's queen-sized bed next to Vee, and at first I didn't remember anything about the night before. My head hurt and my mouth was dry and I had a real stiffness, an ache, in my arm, but as hangovers go, this one was mild, and it was kind of nice being there in that bed with a warm body next to me. I pulled back the covers and swung my feet onto the floor. Behind me, Vee rolled from her side onto her back, and I looked at her, her right arm flung over her head, her hair a pool beneath her, her beautiful breasts exposed. And half of her face like a giant blackberry.

It came back to me then all right. It was like all of the air had been sucked out of my body. I remembered the teardrop of fire that Vee had set down on Joe's bed, and it made me shudder. I got up and stumbled into the bathroom, turned on the cold faucet in the sink as far as it could go, cupped my hands beneath it, and brought them to my face. The water hit the basin with such force that it splashed my chest as well, getting my undershirt wet. I repeated the process over and over, cupped hands, splash on the face, until my fingers were numb and my shirt was soaked. I turned off the water, and used the sink to prevent me from collapsing.

In the mirror I watched the water run off the end of my nose and chin. My eyes were frightened. I looked haggard, but I had looked that way plenty of mornings in my drinking days. Hell, I still looked that way most mornings. But my eyes... I made myself look even closer, to see where it was written that I had killed a man, my own son, and burned his body. All I saw was the fear, and that I needed a shave.

I stood up and pulled the wet shirt over my head, using it to wipe off my chest. The room around me had receded, my insides felt shrunken, my hearing was muffled. I needed to get out. If I stayed in the room, I'd just stew. If I woke Vee, she'd be no comfort, just pissed off that I had woken her. I went back into the bedroom and picked my pants up off the floor where Vee had left them when she had undressed me the night before. They were still weighted down by my wallet and keys and the belt threaded in the loops. I pulled them on, and went out into the living room where I had hung my clothes in the coat closet. I found a new shirt, and put it on without an undershirt, and dug out some fresh socks from my duffel bag, got my shoes on, and went out into the hall.

The light in the hall was the same, the eternal non-day of electric lights lit twenty-four hours. I needed coffee. I needed a drink. I needed both. I took the elevator down, and stepped into the lobby, where somehow a normal morning was progressing, people coming out of the dining room, checking out at the desk, the doorman helping an elderly woman into a taxicab out front, some men sitting with the morning paper and a cigarette in a clutch of couches and easy chairs. I felt as though I were watching a play I didn't care for. I wanted to scream at them, to tell them they were banal, that their lives would end, and what meaning did they have? How unnatural to sit in a building thirteen stories high made out of materials we couldn't name and couldn't say how they were made, in a block of pavement and concrete that someone had had to lay down, where once there had been only nature, and the few people hunting and fishing, just getting by. And sure, having wars. They killed each other too. But they couldn't conceive of this, a hotel in a city. Yet somebody had, and it was so audacious as to be beyond comprehension.

But I had to look normal. Natural. A little disorientation was okay; I had a hangover. But nothing was terribly out of the way. I'd feel better once I had some coffee anyway. And the thought made me think about money, how to pay, and I remembered the telegrams I had sent yesterday—could that have been only yesterday?—and I thought I'd better check to see if there'd been any reply, that's what I would normally do. Right? Of course it was.

I went to the front desk. The concierge was helping with the morning checkouts, so he was the one who said, "Mr. Rosenkrantz, good morning." His eyes flicked behind me for a moment, at least I thought they did, and he made this odd little nod.

"Morning. Do I have any telegrams waiting for me? I'm expecting a couple."

His eyes looked at something behind me again, but he had a broad smile on, and said, shaking his head, "No. No telegrams, sir."

It was bugging me the way he kept looking behind me, like I wasn't interesting enough to hold his attention, so when I turned around and there were two men in dark suits almost right behind me, I was surprised. I really was.

"Mr. Rosenkrantz," the one on the left said. He was heavyset, a bit of a potbelly, rounded cheeks, with tufts of orange hair showing beneath his hat.

"Yes?" I said, looking back at the concierge as if for help.

"Sir, I wonder if you would come with us?"

My stomach dropped and my headache started pounding. It made it really difficult to think. "I don't understand," I said.

"We have news," the other one said. He was like a movie star, strong jaw, dark brow.

"We're Calvert PD," the orange-haired man said, and I hoped my face didn't show anything, even as my whole body felt deflated.

"If you'd just step to the side here, Mr. Rosenkrantz. We want to have a little talk."

Just to the side. They weren't taking me to the station. They weren't arresting me. "I don't understand. What's going on?" I wanted to stall. As long as I was near the desk, the concierge was still part of this, and it couldn't be too bad.

"Mr. Rosenkrantz, please." The heavyset man took a step back and held his hand out to indicate that I should go ahead.

I went. I didn't like to, but what else was I going to do. They stayed behind me, but the redheaded man stayed a little to my side, so I could see him out of the corner of my eye.

"This is fine," he said, as we came to a support pillar

with a large potted plant beside it, and we stopped and I turned towards them.

"Sir," the redheaded man said. "I'm Detective Healey and this is Detective Dobrygowski."

I looked from one to the other, unseeing, but at the same time hoping that I looked appropriately responsive, the way an ordinary person would if confronted this way.

"It is with great reluctance and sympathy that I have to inform you that your son has passed on."

"What," I said, blinking rapidly. "What do you mean passed on? I saw him yesterday."

"I'm sorry, sir, it's always the hardest thing to tell people."

"I don't get it," I said, shaking my head, floored. I mean, I knew it before he said it, but hearing him say it was a whole different thing than carrying Joe's dead body up the stairs. It made it impossible to deny. "What happened?"

Dobrygowski started, "We won't know for certain until after an autopsy—"

I cringed at the word.

Detective Healey took over. "It appears as though he fell asleep with a lit cigarette and the bed caught fire."

As he said it, he watched me carefully, and that made me shudder, but I figured that was okay. When you lose someone close to you, people act in all kinds of crazy ways, so I figured I was clear no matter what I did, but that didn't stop it from worrying me. Still, Vee's plan had worked. That was some relief.

"We were wondering if you could maybe fill in a little

of what happened last night, just for our records," Detective Healey said.

Dobrygowski pulled a pad out, and I shivered again.

"I don't…"

"You were there last night. At the house, weren't you?"

"Yeah, sure. I mean, I got to the house, but Mary," I looked him in the eyes, "she's Joe's fiancée, they're getting married," his lips turned down ever so slightly at the present tense, and that was good. "Mary was leaving, said Joe didn't want to be bothered."

"So you didn't go inside? You didn't see your son?"

I shook my head, stalling for time, while not exactly saying no. My heart was going fast, and my headache was pounding, making the whole room look dull.

"Because Miss O'Brien said she called your son around midnight, she thought…" Healey looked at Dobrygowski, who nodded, and then Healey looked back at me. "She said you answered the phone."

I froze. I'd forgotten that call. I hadn't even told Vee about that call, and it's a good thing I hadn't, because she would have left me to rot.

"Mr. Rosenkrantz. Isn't that right? Didn't you pick up the phone when Miss O'Brien called?"

I didn't like the way he said that, like I'd been caught in a lie. But I nodded and hoped I still looked shocked, not frightened. "Yeah. I did. I went back. I didn't go into the house that first time, but I went back, maybe an hour later."

"So that was around midnight?"

"If you say so. I didn't look at the time. I was drunk."

And I looked down, as though I were sheepish about admitting I'd been drunk.

"So you got there around midnight, and you left?"

"I don't think I was there more than half an hour. But why is this important?" And I was surprised to suddenly find tears in my eyes.

"We just like to establish a timeline. It won't take another minute. Can you go on?"

I blinked my eyes and swallowed. I was really tearing up. And it's a good thing I was, but to think that I had more crying in me. I nodded.

"So you went to see your son, but Miss O'Brien was there, so you left."

"She said he didn't want to see anyone, and I walked down the steps with her. We left at the same time," I said as a tear fell down my face. I pulled out a handkerchief and wiped my face.

"I'm sorry to put you through this, Mr. Rosenkrantz," Healey said.

Dobrygowski didn't look sorry. He just had his pencil poised over his notebook.

"No, it's good, I understand. I want to know what happened too. That's my...Joe's...it's my only child." I hoped that wasn't laying it on too thick, but it was true, and I was really feeling it. I really was.

"So you went back around midnight..."

"I went back. We talked for a little bit, drank. He was drunk, I was drunk, and I left."

They didn't seem particularly impressed with this story.

"If you want to know the truth, he sort of threw me out," I said. "Our relationship wasn't always very good.

He blamed me for the divorce always. From his mother."

"No, we understand. That's all the same as Miss O'Brien said. I'm sorry to even have to put you through it at a time like this. It really makes us heels, and I hate to do it."

"It's all right."

"It's not all right, but it's the way it is."

I nodded.

Dobrygowski spoke then. "But why did you say at first that you hadn't gone into your son's house?"

Healey gave him an angry look, but somehow I got the sense that it was a staged look, that I wasn't quite out of the woods yet. Maybe I wasn't even close to the edge.

"I didn't say I didn't go in. I said I didn't go in that first time. I went in the second time, like I told you."

"It just seems a little weird to me that you would say you didn't go in, when you did."

"I said I didn't go in that first time," I repeated. My tears were gone. I felt worn.

"Leave it be, Pete. Man just lost his son."

Dobrygowski closed up his pad and put it in his inside pocket. "Of course, I'm sorry. Just the detective in me."

"You don't think that there's any…I mean, that some-body…did…something?" I said.

The question actually seemed to relieve Healey. I guess that's the kind of question people ask right up front in cases like these.

"No, no," Healey said. "Forget Dobrygowski. We know you didn't mean anything. But, one last thing. Miss O'Brien said you were here, but you're not registered. I was just wondering…"

"I'm staying with…a friend."

"Yeah, it was just odd when you weren't registered, that's all."

I burst a little then. "Why's it odd? I'm a well-known writer. Sometimes it's better if people don't know where I'm staying. There are some crazy people out there."

Healey paused before responding. "You don't have to tell us. We didn't mean anything by it."

"I just don't like the way this one's asking me about whether I went into Joe's house or not when I said I did. And Joe was fine when I left. Drunk, but fine."

Healey held out both his hands to calm me. "We didn't mean anything by it. We know this is a tough thing. We just like to make things clear."

I knew I had tripped up then, getting angry like that, but you don't know what it's like when you have the police there and they're asking questions just about something you don't want them to know. "Well, I don't like the implications that you think I'm lying or hiding something. My son just died."

"We know, Mr. Rosenkrantz. We're sorry."

I rubbed my head, trying to push out the headache. "And you ought to be."

Dobrygowski said, "You'll stay in town until after the funeral now, I take it."

Healey looked at him like he could kill him.

"What are you suggesting," I started, both hands to my temples now.

"Mr. Rosenkrantz!" A woman's voice, and we all three turned. It was Mary, and as soon as her eyes met mine, her face crumpled and she started to cry. I stepped forward, and she was in my arms, her own arms wrapped around me, crying into my chest.

I looked at the detectives over her head, and even Dobrygowski looked embarrassed. They walked away, and I brought my lips to the top of Mary's forehead, kissing her, letting her know everything was all right.

11.

We held each other for a full minute, which was long enough for me to think about the fact that we hadn't known each other until the day before, and then—and yeah, I feel guilty about it—that her small young body felt good against mine.

"Those were the policemen who came to our house this morning," she said, still pressing her head against my chest.

"It's a hard job," I said.

"Mommy and Daddy were just impossible, bringing me tissues, and a glass of water, and looking at each other over my head, and walking around like I was going to break, I just had to get out of there."

I ran my hand along the hair at the back of her head. "It's okay."

"I knew we had plans for this morning," she said, her voice cracking, becoming almost a whisper. "I wanted to make things all right with you for Joe." The crying got worse again, but she was able to pull herself together quickly this time, even if she still held on to me.

If you think you've ever been in a tough place, you can't even imagine what it was like holding that little girl, as beautiful and sweet as anything, knowing I had murdered her true love. You can't even know.

She pulled back a little, just enough to raise her head so she was looking up at me, but I still had my arms around her, and I was starting to feel excited about her, so close to me like that. "Don't say I have to go back to them, Mr. Rosenkrantz. I can't stand another minute of pity, not today. I just need to grieve without feeling like I'm putting on a show."

"Sure. You can stay right here with me. Or go anywhere you like."

"It's just that I knew you'd be grieving too. It's different when the other person is grieving too." The tears filled up her eyes. "Oh, damn me. All that time this week I tried to be there for Joe while he was mourning. No wonder he was angry. He probably hated me every minute."

"Of course he didn't. Hey, how could he hate you? He was going to marry you."

"Yeah." Her eyes turned down. "I know. It's only just that it didn't *feel* like he was going to marry me anymore. You know? It was kind of like I'd lost him already when Quinn," her eyes darted to me to see how I would take that familiarity, "when she died. And now I know why."

I pulled her against me again and patted her back. "Shhh."

"I'm sorry. You're grieving too."

"Shhh. What do you say to some coffee? Do you want to get some coffee, maybe something to eat?"

She shook her head, rubbing her face on my chest.

"Should we go somewhere? You need some air."

"I just need to lie down."

"Okay," I said. "Sure. We can go up to my room if you

think that's okay. I just need to go up and…see that everything's all right."

She wiped her cheeks with her hands.

"Can you wait for me a moment? Will you be okay?"

She nodded, blinking her tears away. "I don't know
why Joe was so angry at you. I told him I was sure you
were perfectly nice, that it was a misunderstanding. I just
knew you were. Anybody who's read your books can see
that."

I'd felt guiltier and guiltier as she spoke until she went
and ruined it with that last bit about my books. Why'd she
have to do that? I wasn't my books. I wasn't even the
person I was when I wrote those books.

"I'll be back," I said. "You wait right here."

She nodded again, and I crossed the lobby to the elevators and hit the call button. The dial over the door
began to run counterclockwise. Away from Mary, my own
grief came rushing back in, and I felt my knees give way;
I had to hold out my hand to lean against the wall. I had
grieved before. When my parents died. When a girl I
knew, an actress in Hollywood, was killed. That had torn
me apart, the violence ripping her away from me. God,
the same thing had almost happened to Clotilde back in
France when a man had surprised her at home. I couldn't
even bear to think of that; I wouldn't have survived if…
And sure, I grieved when Quinn died. But this was different. The guilt echoed over the grief, the two trading
off of one another, and it was all I could do to get on the
elevator and hit the right button for our floor. I leaned
against the wall inside, and let myself be carried up.

Upstairs, I stepped out of the elevator, and turned

towards our room—Vee would understand if I brought Mary up even if she didn't like it—but ahead of me in the hall Carlton Browne stepped out of our room, stopping, stepping out of the way while looking back, and then Vee stepped out in a red dress and sunglasses. I dropped back, and managed to catch the elevator door just as it was closing. I stepped inside, hit the button for the lobby, and then jammed the button to close the doors repeatedly until the doors slid shut, and with a gentle jerk, I started down again.

My heart was pounding. I didn't know why exactly. I was sweating. And it dawned on me, I was afraid. I was scared to death of this gangster Browne. I didn't know how much more my nerves could take, between Joe and Browne and Vee and Mary and now the police and even Great Aunt Alice who was no doubt still waiting for me to drop by, maybe now more than ever since Joe was gone.

The door opened and I hurried to Mary, putting my arm around her before she could even say anything, and leading her back to the elevator. With luck we wouldn't have to see Browne or Vee at all. But the counter for the elevator I had gotten out of was climbing, while the other counter fell, paused for a moment, and then fell again.

I pulled Mary closer to me as the doors opened, and Browne and Vee stepped out right in front of us. Vee was hidden behind those sunglasses, which covered most of her bruise, but certainly not all of it; I couldn't make out her expression. Browne saw me, and his lip curled in a snarl at first, but then he laughed, and put a hand on my shoulder.

"Vee, look, it's your cousin." He looked at Mary. "With

his very lovely young friend. You making this girl cry, cousin?"

Vee took his arm before I could say anything. "Carlton, please. You promised."

"I'm just saying hi," he said back at her. He gave Mary another hungry look. "You do okay for yourself, bud." He looked back at Vee to see how she was taking this, and laughed again, a mean laugh. Then he gave my shoulder a painful squeeze, and walked past us, Vee trailing him. She didn't even look at me, which was good.

I ushered Mary into the elevator. I exhaled. I had been holding my breath, it turned out, and I felt lightheaded. The doors closed, we started our ascent, and all of a sudden I felt as though I were going to cry.

I must have looked it, because Mary put her hand to my face. "I'm so thoughtless, doing all of the crying."

I pulled my face away from her, and shook my head with my lips pressed tight, holding in my tears. I would have them bring me up a bottle of whiskey, damn sobriety, my son had just died.

She drew her hand away, uncertain of herself, and then the elevator door opened. I led her down the hall to Vee's and my room. We went in, and I guided her to the couch, where I sat her down. "Wait," I said.

I went to the door and put out the Do Not Disturb sign, and then I went into the bedroom where the bed was still unmade—had Vee and Carlton only just gotten out of it? I pushed the thought away—I went into the bathroom, ran the tap until the water ran cold, filled the glass and brought it back to her. I handed it down, standing over her while she drank, like a parent tending to a sick child. When she'd finished, she handed it back to me, looking up at me with timid eyes, and I set it on a glass coaster on the coffee table.

She turned to her clasp bag, which I hadn't even noticed until then, and then stopped and looked up, and said, "Is it all right if I smoke?"

"Of course," I said. "You want a drink too?" I picked up the telephone receiver.

She shook her head, got out a cigarette packet, pulling the box of matches she had stuffed in the cellophane wrapper and then shaking out a cigarette and placing it between her lips.

The desk picked up. "Could you send up a bottle of whiskey? Any kind is fine. Thanks." They'd probably send me the most expensive bottle in the place, all hotels are chiselers, but that was all right with me. If Vee and Browne were all patched up, then the whiskey was on Carlton. I'd like a good whiskey. And just the thought of the alcohol coming on up relaxed me.

Mary blew out a stream of smoke. "I was so happy last night when you answered the phone at Joe's and said you'd made it up."

I nodded, trying to remember if I had said that.

"Why had you fought? Joe never wanted to talk about it. It just made him angry, so I tried to not bring it up."

"Why are you here instead of with your parents? With some stranger."

"You're not a stranger. You're Joe's father."

"But I am a stranger. You don't know me from anyone

else. And I could be just as horrible as Joe thought, couldn't I? Sure I could. You don't know. So why are you here instead of with your folks?"

"I told you I couldn't stand to be with them right now." Her voice was flat, and she took a jerky drag off her cigarette.

"But why?"

"I just— They were on my nerves. I— Oh, do we have to talk about them?"

"Yeah, well I guess that's the same reason Joe hated me."

"He didn't hate you."

"Sure he did. Did it hurt? Of course it did. But I had to get used to it. I had to like it."

"But you made it up last night," she said, and pulled on her cigarette for punctuation.

"Right. Of course, we made it up last night," I said. Well, we had certainly ended it, whatever it was.

She stared straight ahead, smoking. "He was the most caring boy I ever met." She shook her head. "He had a temper. He'd get mad real fast, but he never got mad at me. For me, he was more defensive than I was for myself."

I listened, and the pit in my stomach grew, every word pulling my throat along after it.

"He was so faithful. He lived for his mother. She could do no wrong. She was the ideal everyone had to live up to. And for some reason he thought I did. When he talked to me, when he would tell me he loved me, it was almost like he was describing someone else, someone I didn't know. It was like he was making me up, and I liked who that girl was. I wanted to be that girl."

I jiggled my knee, and couldn't get it to stop. She was conjuring him now, someone I had never known, and it was making me sick.

"He wrote poetry. He'd probably be angry at me for telling you that. He didn't want anyone to know. He assured me it was okay, because it wasn't fiction, he was so afraid of being at all like you. He never drank, too."

There was a knock at the door. I went for it, relieved at the interruption. A bellboy stood there with my whiskey, a brand I didn't recognize. I found a quarter in my pocket and gave him his tip. He was a professional, and made no indication as to what he thought of the amount.

I brought the bottle of whiskey back to the couch and pulled the glass I had served her water in closer to me. "It's the only glass," I said by way of explanation as I twisted off the top, and sloshed out a good dose of alcohol. I held it out to her, but she just shook her head, blowing out smoke, her cigarette more than halfway gone, so I downed the whole thing in one burning go. It sat heavily in my stomach, but it warmed me up, and I felt easier immediately. I refilled the glass, and sat back, taking more reasonable sips. If Mary hadn't been there, I probably wouldn't have bothered pouring it into a glass.

"Does it stop?" she said.

"No. But you think about it less. And the edge gets dulled."

She shook her head. "I'm so tired."

I sighed, and drank.

She looked at me. "So very tired." Her face was completely drained of color.

I drank some more. "You should sleep then," I said.

She ground out the stub of her cigarette in the ashtray on the table beside her. "No…"

I stood up, indicating the couch. "Come, lie down. Sleep. You'll feel better."

"I couldn't sleep last night I was so worried." There was a break in her voice, the tears about to come again. "He… We were going to be married." And a sob escaped her.

I felt as though I had been stabbed. The searing pain of the night before when Joe stabbed me with the ice pick flashed through my chest even as the pain in my arm was nothing more than a soreness now. I could have killed myself right then. All the guilt I'd ever felt over the years had never been like this. I thought of the policemen's suspicions this morning—but had they been suspicious? was it just in my mind?—and I wanted to come out and say it. To say that I had killed him. That I should be punished. But of course I didn't. And I wouldn't. I was too much of a coward.

I picked up the bottle, poured myself a glass, and tossed that one back too, pouring the next one while still swallowing. It was helping calm me at least. "Lie down," I said.

"No," Mary said, while lying down anyway.

I brought her a blanket from the closet, and draped it over her.

She reached out with a hand and pulled it closer to her chin, rocking once back and forth. "You look so much like him," she said, looking up at me.

I smiled. "Thank you."

"How am I going to live?"

I could ask myself the same thing. But I said, "Close your eyes."

She did, and she was asleep within moments. I sat and drank and made an active effort to think of nothing but pouring the liquid from one container to another and then into me. It was a lucky break, Carlton seeing me with Mary and thinking she was a girlfriend. I don't know if Vee knew who Mary really was or not, but I hoped if she was angry, she was at least a little relieved at being in the clear with Browne. That wouldn't help her face, she would have told me, and I wouldn't have had anything to say to that, but it was something.

I thought of Mandy. She was the girlfriend in Hollywood who had gotten killed. We'd been...dating, we'll call it, for a few months when it happened. We fought all the time we weren't in bed, although I couldn't tell you what we fought about. And it had Clotilde out of sorts with me too since I was never too good at keeping anything secret. (Only I'd have to keep this secret, Joe, this one thing.) Then Mandy was murdered by some madman they never even found, and I discovered her body all cut to ribbons, blood everywhere. It was the worst thing I'd ever seen, and I'd dreamt about it a long time after. Was this going to be like that?

Clunk—he went down—clunk—he went down—clunk.

Of course it would.

I poured another drink, and drank it down. My stomach began to feel full, but I was calm, able to think on it and stay calm. Mary slept silently on the couch. She slept with such trust, I wanted to get her up and get her out of there, to tell her to stay far away from me, that I was no good, she didn't need to know why, but Joe was right, I was a terrible person, and she should keep away.

It hit me that Joe had been visiting when Mandy was killed. No, wait, that couldn't be, because I'd really gone on a drinking binge after that, enough so I remembered it. And that was when Clotilde…when she first went to the hospital. So Joe hadn't been there. But he'd met Mandy. I'd practically handed him off to her like she was a babysitter. And Quinn let me have him at all. I was no good even then. Yeah, he had been right to hate me. Here's your kid. Why don't you leave him with your mistress so you don't have to stop getting drunk? I could have killed him any number of times, I was so irresponsible. But he had been the one to hit me at his high school graduation. Hell, he had stabbed me last night. But…

Clunk—he went down—clunk—he went down—clunk.

I needed to do something. The whiskey was good, and it helped, but I needed to do something. I couldn't just sit there thinking about it, not if I didn't want to go crazy. Mary slept on. Should I leave her? Where should I go?

And I don't know why it came to me. You probably won't believe it if you try. But I thought, I should write something. I should do some writing. I hadn't done that in who knows how long. That was what I needed.

I retrieved the pad, and this time I found a pencil in the back of the desk drawer. It had gotten lodged in a small space between the back of the drawer and its bottom, so it hadn't rolled around when I opened the drawer the day before. I took the pad and the pencil back to the easy chair I had been sitting on. I balanced the glass of whiskey on the armrest, and I sat staring at the page.

Clunk—he went down—clunk—he went down—clunk.

And I started writing, whatever came into my head. I wrote and wrote and wrote, and I filled up most of that pad, and I finished the bottle of whiskey. I wrote, but don't ask me what I wrote, because I don't know. It probably didn't make any sense, but I wrote it all down anyway, and I think there was something about Joe in there, and I don't know what else.

Mary slept, and I wrote, and Joe was dead.

My hand started to cramp and I wore out the pencil's lead and had to find another, which took me a few minutes, but then I found one just under the edge of the couch, where it must have rolled off the telephone stand. But I filled up pages like I hadn't been able to in years, just pouring it all out, the anger at being washed up, the hate for the people who had done it to me, the fear for Clotilde, and all the goddamn YMCA rooms, and living with a whore, and just all of it, all of the meanness that had settled inside of me since Clotilde went away, hell, maybe before then, maybe from when Quinn and I started fighting. Yeah, I'd always gotten a raw deal, and I was too pathetic to do anything about it, and I hated myself for that. I hated myself and every goddamn one else, every last one of them.

12.

It was only when I woke up that I knew I had fallen asleep. Someone was moving in the bedroom, and the sound of drawers opening and slamming shut had seeped into my dream and woken me. My watch said two o'clock. Mary was gone. She had draped over my legs the same blanket that I had draped over her that morning. The pad I had been writing on was still in my lap under the blanket, but the pencil was gone.

I listened to the hurried sounds in the other room for another minute, working up the energy to get up. I knew it was Vee and I had a pretty good idea of what she was doing and I wasn't ready to deal with it just yet, to deal with her after last night. My shoulders and back ached from sleeping in a chair for too long, and when I stood up, everything went black for a moment and I thought I'd lose my balance, but the black resolved itself to white patches, and then the room came back into focus.

I stepped over to the entryway into the bedroom. Vee was stuffing things into a suitcase with bitter violence. "Vee," I said, my voice coming out in a croak.

She yelped, and brought her hand to her chest. "Jesus H. Christmas, Shem, you scared the bejeezus out of me. What the hell's the matter with you?"

"What are you doing?"

She went back to it. "What does it look like I'm doing?"

"Where are you going?"

She stormed around the bed to the vanity where she started collecting her makeup and perfume. "Carlton wants me upstairs in his suite. He wants to keep an eye on me, no thanks to you."

The makeup was zipped up in a carrying case and brought over to the suitcase on the bed.

"You better start packing too," she said. "You're thrown out."

My lingering exhaustion deepened, my shoulders sagging. "Where am I supposed to go?"

"I'm lucky he hasn't killed me," she said, pulling some shirts on hangers out from the armoire. "I just wish he'd send me home. I'm not too keen on sticking around."

"Where am I supposed to go?" I said again.

She looked up at me. "Quit whining! You start whining, I'm going to beat your head in myself, getting me mixed up in a murder, getting me in hot water with Carlton…" She was so angry, she didn't even know how to finish. She stuffed shoes into the suitcase, forcing them into a corner on top of some clothes. "I don't know why I even helped you," she said, and paused in her packing, sneering at the suitcase. "I'd say something about love, if I didn't know that was just a crock."

I felt sick to my stomach, or I had heartburn, or both, and I was suddenly very hot and clammy.

"Why aren't you packing!" she yelled. "Start packing. You've got to be out of here toot sweet."

"I feel sick," I said. How had I looked with loving calm on this no-good woman only that morning as she slept?

"What does that have to do with the price of tea in

China?" She was trying to close the suitcase, leaning on it with all of her weight.

I retrieved my duffel, my mind dead as I did it. In the mirror on the front of the bathroom door I looked like I had a hangover and had slept in my clothes, which was how I should have looked, and it wasn't any great surprise, I'd looked that way plenty of times before.

"Vee," I started, but she cut me off.

"Don't say 'I love you,' I just told you love's a crock, and only foolish little girls believe any different, and I'm not a foolish little girl, so you can just hold any sentiment, it's not going to buy anything with me." She crossed her arms over her breasts, and her face grew narrow. "Besides, you love Chloë, and you always have and always will, calling every day to check on her, begging me to take you across the country so you can pay for her precious hospital. You sponger, you bastard, don't you dare say anything to me."

Her suitcase was still open, and she hit it, and said, "I hate this thing."

I knew I needed to say something, but my mind couldn't catch on what it was I was supposed to say. "I guess I'll stay with Great Aunt Alice," I said.

Vee stamped her foot, and then clopped around the bed, heading past me to the bathroom.

"Vee, I'm sorry," I said, panicked all of a sudden that she wasn't just leaving me until we could get out of this situation, but that she was leaving me for good, and I couldn't live with that. I grabbed at her shoulder, and she shook off my grip, but didn't go into the bathroom. "Please," I said.

She turned, and said, "No, you comfort me this time," and she fell into my arms.

"Shhh," I said, and patted the back of her head. It was the second time that day that I'd found myself in that position, a girl in my arms, but I still didn't know what to say, so I said, "It'll be okay."

"No it won't. Carlton's going to kill me," Vee said.

"He's not going to kill you."

"He's not, huh?" She pulled back so I could see her bruised face. "This was just a love tap?" And then she put her head back on my chest. "You better be getting a good share of that money now, with your son out of the way."

I stiffened.

"You talk to the lawyer yet?" she said.

I pushed her away from me, and turned to get my clothes out of the closet in the living room.

She followed me. "Oh, I repulse you now? I'm a gold digger?"

I didn't say anything, but walked around her and stuffed my clothes into my duffel. I don't know why I was angry at her for asking about the money. I certainly had no right to be.

"Well, did you go to the lawyer?" she said, putting her hands on her hips.

"No."

"You better."

"I will."

"You better, that's all."

"Didn't I just say I will?" I said, spreading my arms in defiance. "How long are you going to be staying with Carlton anyway?"

"I don't have much choice in the matter."

"Damn it, how long are we going to be *stuck* here?"

"Do you get the money?"

"I don't know."

"Then I don't know how long we're going to be here. Until Carlton gets bored with me, I guess. That's usually four or five days. Don't you have to go to the funeral anyway?"

The funeral? What funeral? Oh, right, Joe's funeral. "I guess I do," I said, and dropped my duffel on the floor.

"I guess I do," she mimicked. She went back to her suitcase and started to struggle with the zipper again. I came around to help her, and she stepped back, and let me take over. I put my weight into it, and the zipper started to move. I had to switch hands to get it to go all the way around, repositioning the pressure from my other hand as I went. It closed and I straightened up, a fine sheen of sweat on my forehead.

I turned to go back around the bed, but Vee stopped me. "I'm just scared," she said.

"Of what?"

"Of Carlton and of getting caught."

"I'll go see the lawyer," I said. "Then we'll get out of here."

"We better get that money."

"I'll call the lawyer," I said again.

She picked up her suitcase, staggered under the weight for a moment, and started across the room. Without looking back, she said, "The room's already checked out. You just have to vacate."

She went out the door. My neck and back muscles

were all tensed, and I tried to relax them. I'd fought with a lot of women, but none who could hang a murder on me, only that part I didn't figure out until later. For now, I was thrown out without any money, and nowhere else to crawl but Great Aunt Alice's, and that wasn't the best position to be in, believe you me. There are always ways in which things can get worse.

13.

Great Aunt Alice's house was one of the old mansions in Washington Hill facing north on the eastern square. There was still a marble stone at the curb from the time when such a step was necessary to descend from a horse-drawn carriage, as there was a wrought-iron boot scraper at the foot of the stone-carved stairs that led to the front door. The house was a three-story townhouse built of Cockeysville marble, the first floor one and a half times as high as the second and third floors, which allowed for large wooden pillars and a small portico above the door. Narrow black shutters framed each of the four windows across the second and third floors, held in place by hammered iron S's.

I had stopped on the way there to get one drink, which had turned into two, and I wondered how long this bender would last. I mean, I was still on the wagon and this was a temporary setback due to circumstances. But the alcohol had bestowed on me a general lightness that allowed me to think it wouldn't be so bad to see Great Aunt Alice, it might even be nice to see a familiar face, and one who called you family even when you weren't. She had always remained a friend to me, remembering me at Christmas and my birthday, and unashamed at chiding me for what my life had become. She was sure to take me in, and could be just what I needed to pull myself together. I pressed the button for the bell, and deep chimes played an eight-note melody somewhere inside, real classy.

Connie answered the door in a frilled apron tied over a black ankle-length skirt and a deep blue blouse. She didn't seem surprised to see me standing there with my duffel bag in hand, some shirts hanging on hangers over my shoulder, she just took it in stride. "Mr. Rosenkrantz. You come in now, come right in."

"Connie, you see," I said, stepping inside, "I was wondering if…"

She closed the door behind me and took my things. "Miss Hadley in the conservatory," she said. "Tea's as soon as I get it heated up. I'm a have to make up a second plate."

"Great, Connie, great, thank you," I said, and smiled my charming smile. "I know my way."

But she'd already turned to take my things up to one of the guestrooms.

The house had the sweet smell of lemon-scented dust cleaner. There were fresh flowers in a brass vase on the marble side table, and the exposed hardwood floor in the hall to the kitchen reflected white patches of light streaming from the back of the house.

I went through the front sitting room, the small dining room, and the sewing room to the open glass door to the conservatory, which ran along the back of the house. Great Aunt Alice sat in a white oversized wicker chair that faced the window to the garden. She had a large open book propped on her lap and reading glasses that she wasn't using hanging from a chain around her neck. At the sound of my entrance, she laid her book flat on her legs, and looked up. "Ah, Shem, Shem. You come to see an old lady, what a life saver."

"Great Aunt Alice," I said and bent down to kiss her on the cheek.

She frowned. "Not sober, I see."

"Not drunk either," I said.

She shrugged, and pointed with an arthritis-bent finger at a round glass-topped table in the corner. "Bring that here, will you, Shem? Connie would do it, but you're here, you can at least make yourself useful."

I went over and lifted the table in both hands and set it down beside her. She worked the book in her lap onto the table, leaving it open at her place. "Sit down, sit down," she said pointing again at another wicker chair. I pulled it a little closer and sat down. "I hope you're prepared to talk about books. I could use a little conversation. Connie and I don't have too much to say to each other. And I absolutely can't get her to read. I try and try, but she just won't touch a thing."

I nodded, Mr. Debonair Literary Lion, the charming smile creaking on my face.

"But first, this horrible business about Joseph. Quinn was enough, but we were expecting Quinn. But Joseph, I'm trying to recover."

I tried to produce the appropriate expression, but I didn't know what that was, and just hoped I looked like a father in mourning.

"I understand you were the last person to see him alive."

I shifted in my chair. "I don't know—"

"Yes, yes," she said, nodding. "Mary told me. What a good girl that Mary is. It's a shame, oh, it's a tragedy, that poor little thing. She comes and visits me once a week you know."

"I didn't," I said.

"You know her?"

"We just met."

"Oh, a wonderful girl. She'll be by this afternoon, I'm sure. So unfortunate. But you were the last to see Joseph."

"I guess I was." Why was she harping on that? It made me nervous, like maybe she suspected something.

She gave me a contemplative look. "You're not fooling me. You're tight. I thought you were supposed to be a teetotaler now."

"I am. I am. This thing with Quinn and Joe…"

"Nonsense. That's no excuse. You look terrible," she said.

"Thanks."

"Well, you do." She gave a single satisfied nod. "So what did he say? Last night?"

"Who?"

"Joseph."

Connie came in then carrying a tray with tea, both hot and iced, and cucumber sandwiches, crackers, and pâté. I took the opportunity to collect myself. Of course Great Aunt Alice wasn't suspicious. Why would she suspect something? It was that kind of paranoia that would get me caught. She was just being Great Aunt Alice.

"Thank you, Connie," she said. "You can just put that over there. Shem will take care of it." She turned back to me. "Well?"

"He was drunk. He…was upset still about Quinn, and angry at me, but I don't know what about."

"You should never have split with Quinn in the first place."

That hadn't taken long. "Are we going to go over this now?"

"Joseph needed a father. A boy should have a man around."

"Thanks for the compliment, but I'm hardly a man."

She nodded. "You said that. I didn't say that. I'm not letting you off any hook." She pointed at the tray. "Hand me that, darling, won't you." I got up, and poured her some tea. "And a lemon slice. Yes, that one." She took the cup and saucer from me, and I sat back down. After a sip, she said, "The whole thing's so terrible. And with you right there." She shook her head again, "No," and took some more tea. "What's happening with that wife of yours, that movie star? She still locked up in the loony bin?"

I gave up pretending and let my face fall. "She is."

"Why is that again?"

"She has psychotic episodes and she's suicidal."

She shook her head again. "You should never have split up with Quinn. And you need money, I can tell that."

I had forgotten just how acerbic Great Aunt Alice could be. But I couldn't help but feel as though I deserved to be put on the spot. "It'll work out."

"If you mean it won't kill you, you're absolutely right. These things happen. There are good times and there are bad times, and when you have a bad time, you just hold your head up and remember that tomorrow's another day, it can always be better tomorrow. Now what do you want? Go on and ask it, if it isn't money."

I ran my hand over the stubble on my face, and crossed my legs. "How do you know…"

"You aren't taking any tea. I'm not going to eat all of those sandwiches."

I leaned forward and made myself a plate.

"Well?"

"I need to stay here for a few days." I looked up to see how she was taking it. "Until the funeral at least," I added. "Then I'll be going back to S.A."

"But you'll need me to pay your airfare for that."

I bit into a sandwich. It was cool and refreshing.

"Of course you can stay. Stay as long as you like. We'll have Connie make you up a room. Maybe if I can watch over you, you won't get into any trouble, and I can browbeat a novel out of you."

My body deflated, I wasn't able to stop it, I collapsed under the weight of it all.

Great Aunt Alice shook her head. "Poor Joseph. Poor poor Joseph. And that girl of his. She won't get anything, since they weren't married."

I hadn't even thought about that part of it, and I had a fresh pang of guilt, but I pushed it away. I needed the money more than Mary did. She would find a new beau in no time, but this was my last chance to settle my debts and start anew. And it had been an accident. I hadn't killed Joe for the money. You could hardly say I killed Joe at all.

"You didn't know him well enough," Great Aunt Alice said. "He was really a sweet sweet boy. You didn't know him, and now it's too late for that, no thanks to you. You're a real bastard, Shem, don't think I ever forget that, but a helluva writer, what a writer."

"I don't know what to say to that."

"Don't say anything. You'd only screw it up. Ask me what I'm reading."

And I did. And she talked nonstop for over an hour. She didn't need my conversation at all. She just needed someone to talk at. Joseph dying didn't change it one bit. I was as good as anyone else no matter what I might feel, and of course I couldn't fool her about anything. She knew how much and what I felt. And this was my price to pay. For staying here, for not staying in touch, for not writing, for running around on my wife, for every wrong I'd ever done. Great Aunt Alice managed to remind me of all of it without ever saying a word. She was the mirror of truth. She was what laid bare my conscience and made it impossible to ignore, because I was always going to be inadequate as a man in her eyes even if I was 'a helluva writer.'

After about two hours of that, it was getting up near dinner time, and Great Aunt Alice said I'd have to excuse her, she needed some time to get ready for dinner, and I should go up to my room too. The alcohol had long worn off, and I felt groggy, wiped out, a diffuse headache sitting on the top of my head like a newsboy's cap.

I went up to my room. It was on the second floor in the rear of the house, canary yellow wallpaper with a pin-stripe pattern, a bed with a white duvet and yellow accent pillows, a nightstand, and a bureau. Connie had hung my shirts and pants in the closet, and emptied my duffel bag into the bureau. The sight of the bed hammered me with exhaustion. I was still working off of a sleep deficit, even with the nap earlier, and suddenly the idea of dinner with

Great Aunt Alice, of the hours ahead of me, made it hard to even stand.

I sat down on the edge of the bed. There was a telephone extension on the nightstand. I remembered telling Vee that I would call Palmer to see about the will, but I knew that calling Palmer was exactly the last thing I should do, since it would make it look like I was so anxious to get the money I didn't even care that Joe had died. That was the kind of misstep that someone like Vee would make after they killed somebody. I was proud of myself for thinking of it, and refraining from making the call. Instead I picked up the phone and dialed the long-distance number to the Enoch White Clinic. My heart rate went up, and I started to sweat. I thought, as I did every day, if I could just hear Clotilde's voice…

It was Nurse Dunn who answered. I called often enough that I knew all of the nurses' voices. "Enoch White."

"Yes. This is Mr. Rosenkrantz. I was hoping to speak to my wife, please."

"It's lunchtime. The patients cannot take phone calls. Phone calls can only be received between two and four in the afternoon."

I looked at my watch. About four-thirty, which made it one-thirty in California. But I needed to talk to Clotilde. I couldn't tell her anything, but it would help me just to hear her. "It's only a half hour," I said.

"Mr. Rosenkrantz, I'm sorry."

"Well, can I talk to Director Philips?"

"He's at lunch too. I can take a message."

I sighed. "Yes, I just wanted to let him know that the legalities are being worked out here, but I will have the money. He shouldn't do anything until I get back to California."

She intoned, "Right. I'll pass it on." She'd taken the same message from me countless times. They all had.

"Goodbye," I said, not wanting to get off, not knowing what I'd say.

"Goodbye," Nurse Dunn said, and rang off.

I replaced the receiver in its cradle, and sat with my head bowed and my hands between my legs. I tried to elicit some emotion by forcing myself to think of Joe's head—clunk—hitting the counter, but I was already too beaten to feel anything about that. Great Aunt Alice had taken it all out of me. Instead I fell back on the bed, and slept through dinner, through the night, and well into the next morning, and even then I was exhausted and didn't want to get out of bed. But Connie knocked at the door to tell me that the police were here.

14.

It was Detective Healey and Detective Dobrygowski, and I don't have to tell you I wasn't happy to see them. Connie was hovering nearby as though she expected the cops to steal something if left unguarded. They were smiling and making an attempt at small talk. I stood for a second on the top step and swallowed. If they were coming to arrest me, they wouldn't be trading pleasantries with the maid. They'd told me yesterday it was an accident, and for all they knew it was an accident. They didn't suspect me of anything. I forced a smile, and started down the steps.

"Mr. Rosenkrantz," Detective Healey said. And with concern, "Are you all right?"

So much for my smile. "I just need something to eat."

"Don't let us stop you." But they didn't move any, and neither did I.

I looked at Connie, and they did too, and she got flustered and turned back towards the kitchen.

Healey craned his neck to peer over my shoulder. "Should we follow?"

"Is this going to take long?"

"No, not long, not long," Healey said.

"We don't want to put too much strain on you," Dobrygowski said, "given your loss."

They both regarded me with blank expressions. There was no way to tell if their sentiments were genuine. I gave up any attempt to hide my exhaustion. As Dobrygowski said, I was in mourning. I should look exhausted and done in.

"Nice place," Dobrygowski said. "Must be better than staying in a hotel." That was meant to be a question, but I wasn't biting.

"The hotel said you gave this as a forwarding address." Healey's brow creased again. "Are you sure you're all right? You don't look so good, Mr. Rosenkrantz."

Dobrygowski added, "Tough night? You sleep okay?"

"I slept too well."

"One of those nights. Sure. You want to shut things out, you just keep to bed so long, dead to the world, as long as you don't dream."

"But you always dream," Dobrygowski said, also looking straight at me.

"Not always," Healey said. "But, yeah, usually. Usually you dream. Did you have any dreams, Mr. Rosenkrantz?"

I didn't say anything. Their whole tone was different from yesterday. If they came by just for amusement, I didn't need to amuse them.

Healey got a guilty look on his face. "I'm sorry, Mr. Rosenkrantz. I know you just lost your wife and boy."

"My ex-wife," I said. I don't know why I felt I had to add that. It was comments like that that would get me in trouble.

"Sure, you lost your ex-wife and son. You've got a lot weighing you down. Sleep like that, it's a blessing. It's nature's way of protecting our sanity when things get to be too much. There are plenty of nights where I wish I could sleep right through, dead to the world."

"How long did you sleep?" Dobrygowski cut in.

"Is that really why you're here?" I said. "There's so little for the police to worry about they have to worry if I had a good night's sleep?"

"No, of course not. We've got some other things to talk about, but when we see a man looking down and beaten, we worry. We just want to help out. That's a policeman's real job anyway. To help out."

We all let that sit for a moment to see if any of us believed it, but none of us were that stupid.

"But you must not have gotten much sleep the night before last, right?" Healey went on. He reached into his inner coat pocket and came out with a policeman's notepad. He flipped it open, paging through. "You said you were at your son's house around midnight, that you were there maybe half an hour, and then you went back to the Somerset. So you didn't get to bed until at earliest one, one-thirty?" He looked up at me with a furrowed brow.

"That's what I said." This was starting to make me nervous. Why were we going back through my statement? That couldn't be a good thing. That could only mean they suspected something. But it was hard to think, tired and hungry as I was.

"That seems about right, the man on the desk that night said you came in around 1:15, so that's about what it would be, right?"

"I don't understand," I said, hoping my expression

showed confusion, not fear. "We went over all of this yesterday. What's going on?"

"Why'd you leave the hotel?" Dobrygowski said.

So they did suspect something. "Aunt Alice offered to put me up."

"Aunt Alice. But she's not your aunt, is she?" Healey said.

"Quinn, my ex-wife's great aunt, her mother's mother's sister. Why is this important? Gentleman, I'm really—"

"And she just now decided to put you up?" Dobrygowski cut in. A real bleeding heart, that Dobrygowski. This guy just lost his son; we better grill him.

I didn't say anything. I was sick to my stomach, that ambiguous feeling that could mean hunger or could mean heartburn. I needed to eat, and I needed a drink even more.

"We're just trying to get things straight," Healey said, the good cop.

"I'm sorry, gentleman, but Joe got killed two days ago. I just can't go through this again right now."

"It's funny how you say Joe got killed," Dobrygowski said, jumping on me. "Because if it was just an accident, falling asleep with a lit cigarette, I would have thought you would have said that Joe died, not that he got killed."

"It's just a way of talking," I mumbled.

Healey sighed. He looked at Dobrygowski, but when he spoke it was to me. "The M.E. says that it looks like your son may have been murdered."

And there it was. A punch in the stomach. It couldn't have hit me harder than if they were putting the handcuffs on me right then. Then I'd know at least. I almost retched, but managed to turn it into a burp, covering my mouth. I tasted stale alcohol.

Dobrygowski reached out as though he were going to brace me.

"Are you okay?" Healey said.

I coughed and swallowed, and shook my head, waving my hand to show I was all right, just give me a second, I'm all right.

"I'm sorry to have to bring you more bad news," Healey said, and I could tell he really was. He wasn't a bad guy at that. He really cared. And my reaction had been the right one, it turned out. He thought I choked out of parental horror. I choked because I felt the noose tightening. "It's not definite," he said. "He had a pretty severe skull fracture at the back of his head. It's possible that he just fell, and it's even possible that it didn't kill him, that he still made it to his bed and lit a cigarette. But it looks suspicious, and so we have to look into it."

"Is that why you're checking my story with the deskman?"

"I'm sorry about that. It's no good. It makes me sick. But we had to come at you with this to see how you took it."

"Well, how am I taking it," I said, angry now. Angry that I was so relieved they *weren't* putting me in handcuffs. And angry because it meant I had been much more frightened than I had thought.

"I'm sorry," Healey said again.

"So what happened? Joe was murdered?"

"We didn't say that. We're not saying that. We're just saying that it's something we need to look into."

So they were just double-checking my story. They didn't suspect me of anything. I was just the last person to see him alive, as they always say in the movies. Didn't mean I killed him. He was my kid. How could I have killed him?

"I'm really sorry we had to ruin another morning for you," Healey said.

"So am I." I said it with a little heat behind it. I was entitled to some anger now.

"You will contact us if you think of anything else?"

I sneered. "Oh, you don't have to worry about that."

My tone seemed to pain Healey, but it made Dobrygowski examine me with more intensity. "Right, then. I'm sorry again," Healey said, putting his pad back in his pocket. "We'll let you know if we find anything."

"You know where to find me," I said, showing that I had nothing to hide. I was right out in the open.

Healey opened the door, and I stepped forward and held it as they both filed through, and then I closed it behind them. When I turned around, Connie was right there, creeping down the hall from the kitchen.

"Someone killed Mr. Joe?" she said.

"That's what they're saying," I said.

"It sounded like they was giving you the third degree. If I'd a known that, I'd a said you weren't here, the no-good police hassling a father in mourning. They should be ashamed." Her indignity was enough for the both of us, hands on her hips, lowered brow, and pushed-out lips. "Well your breakfast is all fixed, so come on back and get something inside you now."

In the kitchen, she took a plate out of the oven with a

towel, and brought it over to the small kitchen table. "You don't mind eating in the kitchen here, do you? Miss Alice takes all her meals in here with me now. The dining room's only for company."

"That's fine, Connie." And it was fine. Scrambled eggs, a link of sausage, hash browns, grits, and a toasted English muffin with a container of jam on the side. It was the kind of meal a man deserved on a morning he was hassled by the police. My stomach was still boiling, but I figured it would calm down once I got some grub in me. I dug in, and Connie went about her business cleaning up, not saying anything. She and Great Aunt Alice could probably go whole days without saying a word to one another.

I ate with relish. Once I got the first taste of egg, I knew that my discomfort was more hunger than heartburn, although there was still some of that too.

I reviewed my interview with the police. I had been by turns exhausted and angry, but I didn't think I'd made any big mistakes. Aside from one or two glances from Dobrygowski, and that crack about me saying 'killed' instead of 'died,' it seemed like what they said it was, a routine double-check of my statement now that they were approaching it as a murder and not an accidental death. And they said they weren't even sure if it was a murder, they were just looking into it. No, I was fine. They didn't suspect me of anything. Why would they? I was Joe's father. I ran through it again, and I still couldn't find any other mistakes. I was okay.

I wanted to call Vee, though, or to see her. I wanted to let her know what was happening. But it was exactly the

last thing I should do, and she would be mad as anything
if I did get in touch. It would call further attention to our
relationship than we wanted. For all I knew at the moment, they didn't even know about Vee, and it was better
all around if it stayed that way. Still, I really could have
used her reassuring voice.

I finished my meal. Connie had left the kitchen, pre-
sumably to check on Great Aunt Alice. I knew I should
probably do the same, but even fortified by the food as I
was, I didn't have it in me for another long session in the
conservatory. I couldn't call Vee, and what I'd really have
liked was to call Clotilde, but it was too early on the West
Coast. The hospital would never put me through to her
even if I claimed it was an emergency. Especially if I
claimed it was an emergency. They wouldn't want to do
anything that might unduly excite one of their residents.

That left me with the long day ahead and nothing to
fill it. Except for thoughts of Healey and Dobrygowski
digging around, narrowing their search, closing their net.
The idea was too much to bear. I yawned and thought I
could really go back to sleep, I was that tired, like the
food had weighted me down and I couldn't even find the
energy to stand up. But I made it back up to my bedroom. I collapsed on the bed, and before I knew it I was
dead to the world.

15.

The next few days passed in much the same way. I woke up some time before noon and Connie gave me a meal in the kitchen. I'd go back to my room, try to pick at a book from Great Aunt Alice's library, and then fall asleep after a few pages and be out until dinner. I only saw Great Aunt Alice at dinner. And then the conversation was only of books and it didn't really matter how much I contributed, Great Aunt Alice could talk enough for both of us, which was all she really wanted anyway. Otherwise, I managed to sleep as much as eighteen, twenty hours a day.

The funeral was scheduled for Thursday, one week exactly after Joe's death. I would have liked it to be sooner —I felt I would be safer with the body in the ground— but once it was declared a murder, the city wouldn't release the body until two days after the autopsy, which put it on a Sunday, which in the police bureaucracy really meant Monday. So the earliest the funeral could have been was Tuesday. But Mary was in charge, along with Frank Palmer, and she wanted to get it just right. She'd gotten very particular as a widow. Only of course she wasn't even a widow since they never were married. I just slept, letting it all happen without me, at a distance, and so I was told the funeral was on Thursday and the funeral was on Thursday.

I saw Mary only once in that time, on Sunday. She came to the house all fired up with the distraction of planning, and said that she was in the midst of all of these decisions—the flowers, the clergy, the eulogy, the obituary, everything—and she was afraid that she had overstepped her bounds. She was afraid I would be angry. I put my arm around her and told her it was all right, it was great, it was the way it should be, and the weight of the whole thing suddenly showed on her face. It went from pinched to slack, and her eyes got shiny, but she didn't let a tear drop. She was a good sport like that. She said again that she wanted to think of me as a dad, and I said I wouldn't like anything better, and she managed a smile at that, even if it was pained, and she left, back to her organization, keeping busy to keep her mind off of it.

When I was awake, however, I couldn't keep my mind off of it. It would creep up on me, Joe's fall, carrying his lifeless body up the stairs, the glow of the lighter... Even if it had been an accident, covering it up was surely a crime, and when your kid got hurt, even if you had nothing to do with it, you felt guilty and thought, if only I had...if only...and here I had everything to do with it. Mary wanted to see me as a father, but it was I who needed a parent. With that thought, I'd roll over and force myself right back to sleep.

There was a phone call with Palmer. I *had* come into money. Since Joe died without a will, the estate was distributed according to the order of succession, first to Joe's kids if there were any and there weren't, and then to Joe's parents, which was me. Surprisingly, I didn't feel one way or the other about the news, and we agreed it was best dealt with after the funeral. I knew I should at least tell Vee that much, but I didn't know what her situation was with Browne, and it still felt too risky to make contact. And every time I thought about calling Clotilde, I couldn't face the idea of having to put off Director Philips once more, or worse, on the weekend, one of the sub-directors.

On Tuesday, I was finally forced out of my lethargy. I was dreaming about the funeral, and the bell tolled, but it wasn't one sonorous note but a stream of notes, up and down. They ran through their sequence again, and I became aware of the room, the bed, the leathery dry interior of my mouth, and I realized the ringing wasn't in my dream. It was the doorbell.

I lay there on my stomach in my suit pants and shirt-sleeves, one arm hanging off the bed, feeling too tired to get up, but awake enough to know I wouldn't be going back to sleep anytime soon. Then there was the sound of Connie on the stairs, and a knock at my door.

"Mr. Shem. There's a man here to see you."

I didn't move. I was so numb to everything that I wasn't even worried it was the cops. They could come and take me for all I cared.

"Mr. Shem? Should I send him away?"

I called, "I'll be right there, Connie." There was a pause, and then I heard her walk away. I pulled up my arm, swung my feet around, and sat on the edge of the bed. Man, did my head feel like it weighed twenty-five pounds. I brought a hand to my forehead to support it. If Vee could see me now… I deserved whatever vitriol she could spew, and she was expert at vitriol.

I pulled myself together and got up. I felt a little light-headed and dizzy at first, but that was to be expected. I rubbed my cheeks to get some blood into them, and they were like sandpaper. I couldn't remember the last time I'd shaved.

From the top of the stairs, I could see a young man in a blue suit with no tie and a gray hat. He was familiar, I knew I should know him, but I just couldn't place him. In the back of my mind a note of panic edged in with the sense that this man knew something about Joe's death. He was linked to it in some way.

He looked up when I was halfway down the stairs, broke into a nervous grin, and hurried off his hat. "Mr. Rosenkrantz." His expression got a little funny as he took in my condition, but what was that to me?

"I'm sorry, I..." I said as I reached the bottom of the stairs.

His face fell a little, but he managed to keep his grin. "Taylor Montgomery, sir."

"Who?" I said out loud. I couldn't remember any Montgomery.

His face fell even further, and he looked down. "Oh, I'm sorry, maybe I shouldn't..." He darted a look at me to see how he was faring. "I knew I shouldn't have come."

Montgomery? It dawned on me. It was the kid from the newspaper who I'd shot the breeze with the day I... That was why I thought of him and Joe. It felt like a year ago. "Montgomery. Sure. Sure. No, the kid from newspaper. It just slipped my mind for a minute."

"Because I could come back. Or if you'd rather be alone..."

"No. It's all right. What can I do for you, Montgomery?"

"I got your address from the hotel. They said this was where your messages were to be forwarded. I hope it's all right. I mean, I know with your son and all… I just wanted to tell you how awfully sorry I am. I just feel terrible."

And he looked it too. It embarrassed me to see how deferential he seemed, how worshipful. I couldn't look him in the eye. "Thanks, kid." I put my hand on his shoulder, and he looked up at me with his chin still tucked in.

"It's all right I came?"

"It's swell you came. It's better than all right. I've been alone too much. Your mind dwells on things…"

He rocked on his heels, uncomfortable.

I put my whole arm around him then. "Come on, come in." I led us into the nearby sitting room. There was a sideboard with a small wet bar, and just the sight of the alcohol made me stand up straighter. I'd been very near a teetotaler since coming to Great Aunt Alice's, but now I had a guest, I could have a drink. I went across to the bar and flipped over two glasses.

He looked around for where to sit, and settled on a delicate colonial couch with two-tone yellow upholstery. He perched on the edge. "It's really okay I'm here…?" he said.

"Of course. Of course. What'll you have?"

"Oh, none for me. I'm fine. I'm just here to pay my respects."

"Don't make me drink alone." And I made us each a Gin Rickey. I crossed the room, handed him his drink, and sat in one of the armchairs, an uncomfortable Louis XIV.

He held the drink in both hands, and stared into it, not drinking. Then he looked up at me with equal parts reverence and embarrassed concern. It was how I'd had the strength to go talk to Joe, that look, and you know where that had led. Remembering that made me shift in my seat. He looked down again. "You probably think I'm crazy. Coming like I have a right to visit you. I'm probably ruining my chance to work with you. You probably won't be staying in Calvert much longer anyway."

"Probably not," I said, trying to remember what he meant, 'work with me.' And it hit me that we had been writing together that night, a play. Me, writing.

"Well even if we don't work more together, it's been a real honor." He met my eyes and his were just beaming, and it really made me feel like the rottenest person that ever lived, him looking at me like I was sacred, and me knowing that I was a philandering alcoholic hack screenwriter killer.

"Yeah, it's been an honor for me too," I said, and took another drink so I didn't have to decide what expression to give to my mouth.

He swallowed, looked for a place to put his glass down, and settled on the floor beside his foot. "I shouldn't even say anything," he said, "but even if we're not going to work together, I brought along something I worked up… if you don't mind, it'd mean a lot to me if you looked at it."

I didn't want to look at it. I was too tired. But there was something in his fawning that made me feel like somebody again. And with just that glimmer of self-worth, I started to think, I wasn't bad. I'd just ended up in a compromising situation. And not for any gain. That was the thing. It had been self-defense. This kid would believe that. He knew I was a good guy. So I leaned forward, and held my hand out for whatever it was he'd written, and said, "Sure, why not?"

His face lit up, and he pulled out his pad from his inner coat pocket, the same pad from the bar. He started to flip through it. "It's just an idea for a scene I think would come at the end of Act I." He handed it over, and at first I just stared at the script unseeing. "It hit me what you were saying about the Furies being mortal. And I thought if one of them killed the other, you see, if one Fury killed another Fury, that would be like a sister killing a sister, and then that's exactly one of the things the Furies punished people for, killing a family member, you know, in the old myths." My face must have changed colors, because he stopped and said, "Mr. Rosenkrantz, are you all right? I'm sorry if, well I knew I shouldn't say anything about the play. My mom would kill me if she knew I was here acting like this with you having just lost your son."

I shook my head and held out a hand when it looked like he might try to get up. "It's fine, it's all right. I want to read it, I do," and to prove I did, I started reading. I could feel him watching me and then looking away and watching me again, but I furrowed my brow and focused on what he'd written. And it was pretty good. It was really good, actually, and I felt some of the excitement I had felt with him in the bar the other day. I finished my drink and balanced the glass on the arm of my chair, and flipped through to the end of the scene. It was only four handwritten pages, but it was really good. "I like it," I said, handing the pad back to him.

His eye opened wide. "You do? I mean, you really do?"

"Yeah, it's a great idea. It's a great way to end the first act."

His smile was open and giddy.

"I'd cut that crying and laughing part at the end there."

He knit his brow and stuck out his lower lip in seriousness, nodding. "Sure, I could see that."

"A small action carries a lot of weight on a live stage. And you have this murder. That's going to be big enough. You just let the other two sisters stare at the body in shock. They lead the audience, you see. Everyone's in shock. Because you *are* in shock when it happens. You're looking down and thinking, this couldn't be, it doesn't—it just couldn't. You're in shock, you see." I realized what I was saying, and I got up to fix another drink.

"I see what you're saying," he said, writing something down. "Yeah, that's better than the murdering sister breaking down, if she just looks at her sister's body, and then the third one looks at her accusingly, their eyes meet, and the murderer runs off the stage, lights out." He was writing the whole while he was talking.

I drank half my drink on my way back to my seat. "And then when the innocent sister seeks vengeance on the murdering sister, then she's only left the choice to do the same thing, to kill her sister, and then she's no better off than the other one. Because really, we're all guilty in the end, right? It's not just one person who's guilty, but everyone, because they let it happen, they made it too."

He wasn't quite following me there, and I wasn't even following myself, I wasn't making any sense. "I like it," he said. "I hadn't thought of that."

"Here give me that," I said, reaching for the pad in order to hide my own confusion. He handed it back to me. "And a pen." He handed me that too. I looked at what he'd just written, and I started to jot some dialogue down. It just came to me:

> *"Don't you accuse me. How dare you accuse me. She would have killed me if she'd had the chance." "Do you think self-defense is an excuse? How many times have we ended a life even when self-defense has been invoked?" "I'll never let you get to me. I'll get to you first." "And that'll be self-defense too?" "It will." "Well you have to get to me first."*

It felt good, the dialogue flowing like that. And you read it now, and I know what you're thinking, that I was trying to make excuses for myself. Only I didn't see that at the time. At the time it was just a play I was writing. And the important thing was that I *was* writing. And not the nonsense I'd written in the hotel the other day, but actual dialogue that fit into a play. Montgomery would take care of patching it all together, like the script doctors that come in and touch up a screenplay after you're finished with it.

I looked up for a moment, and saw that Montgomery was watching me with fierce intensity. It made me self-conscious, and I lost the flow of what I was writing. I handed back the pad and mixed myself another drink. He looked at what I had written and then immediately started writing something else down. I watched him work and it was exciting to see his enthusiasm and self-confidence. I wondered what had happened to my own self-confidence.

If only I had a young man like that with me, I'd be unstoppable again.

And then I found myself wishing again that Montgomery had been my son. I would have been a different person with a boy like that looking up to me like I was king of the world. With a son like that you could really make something of yourself. You just about had to with a son like that, because he had you so great that you'd bend over backwards to prove he was right. But Joe had said that he thought the world of me as a kid, and what did I do? I made him think I was worse than I was and it seemed like I had proven him right in the end too.

But that didn't matter. What mattered was that I was up and awake and my mind was sharp.

He started talking. I offered him a drink, and he waved it off, and went on about another plot point in the play, and then we really were working again, just like the night in the bar. Everything else fell away. All of my guilt, my anxiety, my self-loathing, those things evaporated in the creative flow of hashing out murder and drama on the stage. It was so much easier on paper than in— But I couldn't think like that.

I kept drinking and finished the bottle. Montgomery nursed the first drink I had given him, learning from his mistake the last time. He took the role of secretary so I didn't have to worry about my handwriting. We hashed out most of the second act in what must have been something like four hours. I'm not sure how long it was. It wasn't dark yet outside, but it was getting there, that late evening summer twilight.

Montgomery filled up his pad at some point, but he

had another one. He'd really come prepared; he was that eager and hopeful. To him, I really was somebody, even if everyone else in the literary establishment had forgotten me, and my call girl girlfriend didn't want to see me, and I owed money all over, and the police were probably going to arrest me any day. No, for him, I was a big-time writer. And we had that perfect give-and-take you need to get something good. I could feel it was good as it was happening. And maybe, I'm not ashamed to say it, maybe I began to believe it too. *The Furies* by Shem Rosenkrantz and Taylor Montgomery! The new smash hit! Yeah, we wrote.

And I didn't once think of Joe or anybody else.

16.

That was Tuesday, and the funeral was set for Thursday. Montgomery and I wrote all that Wednesday with only two notable interruptions that I guess I should mention. The first was a letter from Vee telling me to meet her at the hotel's luncheonette first thing Friday morning. She didn't know when she could get away so I was to just go and wait. Then we could figure out what we were going to do, and get the hell out of Calvert.

The second was two phone calls back to back, so if you count that as two things, then I'd have to say three things happened that Wednesday. The first phone call really threw me for a loop. Connie announced that someone was on the line for me, and I ran upstairs to take it in my room, expecting that it was Vee and I would need some privacy. But when I picked up, a familiar man's voice came through the line, "Shem Rosenkrantz, I can hardly believe it's you."

I sat heavily on the bed. "Hub." Hub Gilplaine was a nightclub owner and pornographer in S.A. who I used to pen smut books for. We'd been friends, but I soured that the second I asked to borrow money. How had he found me?

"Shem, how long have we known each other?"

"A lot of years," I said.

"A lot of years. So you know what I hate more than anything, don't you?"

"For someone to waste your time."

"For someone to waste my time. That's right. So how come I find out that you've skipped town and I've got to waste precious hours getting you tracked down?"

"Hub, I haven't skipped town. Quinn died, and then Joe—"

"How come?" He'd raised his voice. Then I knew it was personal. He never raised his voice.

I was silent.

"Huh?" He waited for me to answer. "How long have we been friends? You're afraid to call me?"

"I'm coming into some money—"

"Money! Money…"

I could hear him shaking his head through the wire. So he was going to take this offended compatriot act through to the very end.

"Shem, I had to put your name out in a lot of places to track you down, and we've already established that my time is too valuable for that. When somebody offered to buy up your debt, I didn't say no. You and I are square as far as money goes. It's not my problem anymore. I've washed my hands of it."

"But, you don't understand, I'm coming into a lot of money. That's why I'm here."

"Then you'll have no trouble paying your new creditors off."

I had no answer for that.

"That's all I wanted you to know," he said, "that you

have someone else to pay back now, Shem. Someone less patient than I've been."

"Hub…"

"I'm sorry, Shem, I gave you all the time I could."

"Sure. Yeah." But he'd hung up.

I put the receiver down and just sat there, unable to get up. All of the energy that Montgomery had brought out in me in the previous thirty-six hours was gone, just pulled right out of me and across the country. Who was I kidding writing a play? I couldn't get away from my life. In America, you got one chance, and if you hit it big then you hit it big, but if you fell, there was no climbing back up. You might as well just die or go off somewhere where you weren't in the way. Yeah, I might have come into a lot of money, but I owed a lot of money too. And now some gangster had bought up my debt… Who knew how much he'd expect from me? There was no pretending. I was on my way out, not up.

But thoughts like that were doing me no good. I picked up the phone again, and got the Enoch White clinic on the line. I asked for Clotilde, and the nurse on the other end got icy and told me to hold on, and then the phone delivered me a voice that was as relieving as the last voice had been frightening.

"Shem, you haven't called."

"I know, baby. I've been real tied up out here. Joe died."

There was quiet, but not quite silence. She squeaked out, "No," and I sank again. She was supposed to comfort me, and now I'd have to comfort her.

"It's okay, honey, listen…"

"Shem, where are you?"

"I'm still in Calvert. The funeral's tomorrow. Then I'll come home."

"I miss you." She was crying, but quietly.

"I miss you too."

"I love you."

"I love you too. Listen, baby, it's going to be okay. I'm getting the money now. The whole thing, the estate. I'll be able to pay Philips. You'll be set up for a long time."

"Oh, Shem, I'm so happy," but she sounded just the same as she had a second before.

"It's all going to be okay now."

"But Joe died?"

"It's okay, honey."

"I miss you."

I sighed. This was actually worse than the conversation with Hub. He'd sent some gangster on my trail, but Clotilde...she tore it right out of me, you know? She emasculated me. All the no-good things I'd done to her. I just needed to lie back and go to sleep and never wake up.

"You'll pay Director Philips now?" Clotilde said. She'd stopped crying, but her voice still sounded small, like a shy little girl's.

"Yes."

"I'm so happy, Shem."

"Yeah." It went on like that a little longer, with the I-love-yous and I-miss-yous. I'd planned to tell Director Philips the good news about the money, but I didn't have it in me anymore, so when I was able to, I let Clotilde hang up. I don't know how long it took me to get up, but I eventually made it back downstairs to Montgomery, and at first I was morose, but after a drink and a half he was able to pull me back into it, and we wrote until late in the evening, and he stayed and we had dinner with Great Aunt Alice and Connie.

The next day was the funeral. It was unseasonably cool thanks to the rain of the previous night. We gathered at the same funeral home where Quinn's service had been held just under two weeks before. Mary and her parents, Great Aunt Alice, and I sat in the first pew, with Connie directly behind us, and Montgomery a row behind her. Palmer Sr. was also there, and some other acquaintances I didn't recognize, friends of Quinn's from her life without me. It seemed that Joseph had had almost no friends of his own or maybe they were just all far away, seeing as how he'd always boarded at school. I half expected Vee to show up too, and I couldn't decide if I was relieved or disappointed when she didn't. I'd see her the next day at the hotel anyway.

In front of our pew, there was a waist-high wooden barrier that separated us from the closed casket and the podium from which the minister spoke. He did a hell of a ceremony, quoting the Bible about how the Lord giveth and the Lord taketh away, to every season, you die in body but live on in spirit, etc., etc. He threw in a bit about Abraham's test with Isaac on the mountain, and tried to make it that God tested us every day, and some trials were harder than others, but we should always trust in God. I guess he brought that up for my benefit, seeing as I was a father robbed of his only child. It was a nice try, but it only made me sick to my stomach.

When he'd finished, a man from the funeral home announced the location of the cemetery and informed us that people outside would be handing out maps to anyone who needed them. The pallbearers, just members of the funeral home's staff, wheeled the casket up the aisle and we all stood to follow it out.

It was then that I saw Healey and Dobrygowski standing in the back of the room. I had really hoped to not have to see them again, and the sight of them there started me sweating. Fortunately, they filed out ahead of everyone else and were gone from the lobby by the time I reached it. But I couldn't shake the feeling that they had come because they knew something, that they had wanted me to see them so that I could stew a little, and would be more likely to make a mistake when they actually talked to me.

I was on edge the entire ride to the cemetery. I didn't even attempt to talk to Mary or her parents. I told myself that the cops were just paying their respects, that there was no other reason for them to be at the funeral. Even the police couldn't be so cold as to arrest a man at his own son's funeral. They probably had already gone back to work. Surely Joe's case wasn't the only case they were working. They felt obligated to make an appearance, but that was all it was, an appearance, and I didn't have to worry about them anymore.

I'd just about gotten myself believing it when we pulled into the cemetery through an enormous granite archway, the wings of a black iron gate folded back into the grounds. The narrow road was just large enough for a single vehicle. The driver of the hearse expertly drove through the winding hills until he came to the Hadley plot. The large family marker, engraved with the umbrella that had made their fortune, was visible from the car, as was a four-foot pile of dirt.

And on the other side of the road, pulled off on the grass, was a black Lincoln with Healey and Dobrygowski standing up against it.

I got out of the car on the opposite side, and reached back to take Mary's hand. My reflection in the car's window—pallid, pinched face, shoulders hunched nervously, rumpled suit—was frightening. I looked like I had a big 'guilty' sign around my neck, and my only luck was that it was my son's funeral, and I hoped the guise of mourning still masked my expression.

I focused studiously on Mary, and even when Dobrygowski gave me a wry smile and a nod, I acted as though I hadn't seen him. We walked between the graves, picking our way up an incline towards the Hadley marker. It was shocking to see how many of the gravestones, even in the old part of the cemetery, were marked with the war years, '43, '44, '45. And all of them with birth dates as much as twenty-five years after mine.

We got to the grave where several folding chairs had been arranged facing the empty hole. Mary hung onto me for support, but I felt as though I could just as easily topple over on her. I hadn't had a drink that morning, and I was feeling shaky.

I poured her into a seat, but continued to stand myself, facing the grave. I could feel Healey and Dobrygowski behind me, watching from their respectful distance. I began to worry that they were allowing me to attend my son's funeral out of courtesy, and were planning to arrest me as soon as it was over. At the thought, my mouth went dry and my chest grew taut, and it was sheer exhaustion that prevented me from bolting. Exhaustion and the knowledge that making a half-hearted attempt to escape two younger men in a cordoned-off cemetery was crazy and would just make my case look worse.

Great Aunt Alice grabbed my sleeve, startling me. She had her cane in the hand that held my sleeve, and Connie had her other arm. "Shem, help me will you?" Her back was hunched, so that she couldn't look up at my face.

I took her arm, and with Connie's help, we guided her to the empty folding chair on the end, leaving two chairs between her and Mary. I insisted that Connie take one, and Mary pulled me down in the other.

The pallbearers, along with two gravediggers in dungarees, worked the coffin onto a set of canvas straps that hung over the grave on a large stainless steel frame. When it was in place the minister began. He had asked me before the ceremony if I'd wanted to say anything, but I'd declined. He invited Mary to say a few words.

She brought out a much-worried crinkled paper from her small handbag, and stood but did not turn, instead addressing the grave. Her voice was thin, and she had gotten through barely a sentence before she broke down in tears. She waved away any help, managed to regain herself, and continued, although I think she left a lot of it out, the writing on the paper was so small and she only spoke for another minute tops.

Hearing Mary bawl like that nearly made me lose it too. I felt like it was kind of my fault that she had to feel that bad, but I bit down and did what I could to not let it bother me. I wasn't going to give the cops the satisfaction of seeing me cry.

When she finished, the minister asked us to rise. Connie and I stood, but Great Aunt Alice stayed seated, her hands propped on the top of her cane. The cemetery workmen stepped forward and began to undo the locks on the canvas straps, lowering the coffin slowly into the ground as the minister talked about dust to dust. The workmen expertly pulled the canvas straps from the grave and moved off to be unobtrusive. Mary continued to cry, and it kept making me feel worse, but I made it. All of the other funereal trappings were just trappings, things I had long ago internalized and drained of feeling.

The minister finished, and went around the grave. The rest of the little crowd broke up, and started to make their way back to the street where the line of cars was still facing further into the interior of the cemetery. Having been closest to the grave during the ceremony, I was one of the last to leave. Palmer had waited for me.

"Shem, it's been a hell of a month. Just a goddamn hell of a month."

"Yes," I said, not knowing what else to say.

"We still need to meet. Could you come around to my office sometime in the next few days? I'd like to sit and talk with you a minute, let you know what's going on with the estate."

"What's going on with the estate?"

"This isn't the place to go into it. It's just what we talked about on the phone. But since Joe died intestate it's not going to be quite as straightforward as it could be. We don't have to meet for long. You think you can swing by?"

"When do you want me?"

"Anytime is fine. Just drop in."

"Okay."

"You'll do that?"

"Okay."

"Good. Good." He paused, and his voice grew much more somber. "Shem, I'm so sorry."

I said nothing.

"It's been a real hell of a month." He clapped me on the back, rubbed once or twice, and then guided me forward with a hand on the back of my neck, leading us out. Healey and Dobrygowski were still by their car watching me, and when Healey saw that I was looking, he gave a little wave.

Great Aunt Alice and Connie stood at the end of the path at the edge of the road. "Shem, are you coming back with me or you going back with the hearse?" Great Aunt Alice asked.

Neither option would move quickly enough to avoid the detectives. The entire entourage had to drive forward before getting to a turnaround where they could head back. I was as good as trapped.

While I stalled, Palmer walked past us towards his car. Mary's parents had her in the front seat of their car, and I saw her father hand her a flask, and it made me feel awfully thirsty.

"Well?" Great Aunt Alice said.

The detectives started towards me, staying on the grass, out of the way of the mourners, but walking along until they were even with me. They stepped between the cars.

"Mr. Rosenkrantz." It was Detective Healey. "A word."

"Oh, enough's enough," Great Aunt Alice said. "If you catch us, you catch us, otherwise you can make your own way."

Healey and Dobrygowski were beside me then. "We won't be long, ma'am," Healey said, but Great Aunt Alice didn't even look at him. He turned to me. "I'm sorry to be doing it like this, Mr. Rosenkrantz. This isn't really the place for it."

"No, it isn't," I said. My stomach was in my throat, but I tried to make my expression fierce.

"It won't take a minute. You haven't heard anything of Miss Abrams?"

"Miss Abrams?" I said, and my shoulders dropped and my knees went weak. They weren't going to arrest me. Not just then anyway.

Dobrygowski gave a little 'huh' at that to show he was amused.

"You were staying with a Victoria Abrams at the Somerset," Healey said.

"Right. Vee." I turned to Dobrygowski, making sure to look him in the eyes. I just needed to be indignant, the way that anyone would be if the cops showed up at their son's funeral. "Maybe you remember all your friends by last name five minutes after you bury your son."

He held up his hands palms out in apology, but he didn't look sorry. "I didn't mean anything."

"He didn't mean anything," Healey said, giving him a chastising look. He turned back to me. "Have you heard from her?"

Up and down the row of cars, engines came to life.

"I haven't heard from Vee," I said, trying to decide how to play this. It was probably best not to deny the relationship, but to deny everything else. "I'm worried. Why? Is she okay?"

"Sure, she's fine," Dobrygowski said. "Just peachy."

"We don't know," Healey said. "We're looking for her."

"What's your relationship with Victoria Abrams?" Dobrygowski said.

"She's my girl—She, we're…We live together." I decided to switch back to anger. "What's this all about? You come out to the cemetery, pester me at my son's funeral, in front of all of my family, my friends."

"You don't really have much family left," Dobrygowski said.

"Listen, you," I said, forcing myself to take a step towards him, all the while my heart beating so hard I could hear the blood in my ears. "I've had just about enough—"

Healey put his hand out as if to block me. "You'll have to forgive Dobrygowski." He looked at his partner. "That was uncalled for."

Dobrygowski gave another 'huh.'

"Did you know that she also goes by the names Nancy Martin and Michelle Grant?" Healey said.

I swung around to face him. "How would I know? I don't know. She did?" It wasn't that much of a surprise that Vee had other names, but I was flustered by the fact just the same.

"We got a pretty interesting rap sheet from Cleveland on her."

I narrowed my eyes. "I don't care."

"Oh, but you might care about this," Dobrygowski said. "Yeah, I'm pretty sure you'll care. When 'Vee' went by Nancy Adams there was a fire in her house. This was in the suburbs right outside of Cleveland." I waited for it. "There was this fire and her husband was killed."

17.

They watched for a reaction to that. "Her husband?" I said, confused.

"You didn't know she was married before?"

"What do you mean before? I didn't know she was married ever."

A horn honked, and I jumped bringing my hand to my chest. The police looked back at the car we were standing in front of just as the car to our other side pulled away. The caravan was moving again. We stepped off onto the grass.

"Look, I need to go," I said. "I can't handle this right now."

"Of course, of course," Healey said. "Just a few more questions. We can take you anywhere you need when we're done."

I didn't like that, but it was probably better to get it over with.

They took my silence for assent. "So Vee, Nancy, Miss Abrams. You didn't know about her husband."

"I just told you I'd never heard of Nancy whatever-you-said or this other name. I don't understand what this has to do with me."

"Please, don't get upset, Mr. Rosenkrantz. I know

you've got a lot on your mind. We're sorry to have to tell
you more."

"I don't understand," I said again, but then I flashed on
it. Vee had used the murder/arson combination before.
How could she be so stupid! I proceeded cautiously. "So
what are you saying? Vee killed her husband and set the
house on fire?"

"There were those who thought that," Dobrygowski
said.

I looked at him, and he gave me a steel look back. I
had been wrong to dismiss him as an oaf. If there was any
danger of being found out, it would come from him, not
Healey. Healey came on with all of the talking, but he
was a good guy at heart. He didn't want to do it. It was
just his job. I knew how that was. But Dobrygowski...I
knew his kind too, they got an idea and they never let go.

"There was some question with the insurance company," Healey went on. "And the police there—it was just
a small town—they just weren't sure, but they weren't
going to give anything to that insurance company, so they
wouldn't get behind the murder theory, and the insurance company paid up and that was that."

"Why are you telling me this?"

"Just that it's a funny coincidence," Dobrygowski said.

"Funny!" I flared, and I didn't care if I was overre-
acting.

Healey put his hand out again to restrain me. "He
didn't mean anything by it, Mr. Rosenkrantz."

"I didn't mean anything by it," Dobrygowski said.

I took deep breaths and tried to count to ten in my

head. If I lost my temper, I was liable to do something stupid.

"You've just become very rich," Dobrygowski said. "That must be some consolation to you."

"What consolation?"

"We spoke to Mr. Palmer," Healey said. "He told us that your son doesn't have a will. That you stand to come into a lot of money. The family might contest it, of course, but that's something."

I had to be careful here. "I just lost my son, and you're talking about money," I said.

"I'm sorry. I know it's crude. It's an unpleasant job."

"So I've heard," I said.

"You didn't know about the money?"

"Palmer just told me now. But not before."

They switched back to Vee.

"So you lived with Victoria Abrams?" Dobrygowski said.

"Why?" I said, narrowing my eyes.

"We just want to establish what she might have to gain."

So they knew. "Yes, we live together. In San Angelo."

"So she could expect to see some money if it came your way."

"She could, but she wouldn't be getting any. She won't be getting any."

"No?" Dobrygowski said.

I crumpled my features into a question. I needed to still look confused. I needed to be stupid.

"Do you know where Victoria Abrams is?" Healey said.

"No, I don't." It was technically true. They weren't asking where she had moved when we checked out. Just where she was now. "Why?"

"Can you believe this guy," Dobrygowski said.

I made as though it had just dawned on me then. "You think she killed my son and set his room on fire?"

There was an uncomfortable silence. "So you have no idea where she is?" Healey said.

And Dobrygowski jumped in, "Did you know her boyfriend was Carlton Browne, a well-known gangster here in Calvert? Her *other* boyfriend, I mean."

"I…" The caravan of cars had turned and was almost upon us on its way back out of the cemetery. "I…I'm sorry, I've told you what I know. And quite frankly, right now, I don't want to know any more of what *you* know."

"Why'd you leave the Somerset?" Healey said.

I stepped towards the road. Great Aunt Alice's car was almost upon us. "Because Vee's boyfriend found out about me," I said, my eyes on the cars.

Healey took a step towards me to try to recapture my attention. "So you think she's with Browne?"

Great Aunt Alice's car was abreast of us now, and slowed. I walked to the rear door, relieved to have an excuse to be done with them.

"Don't you want to know what happened to your son?" Healey said behind me.

I jerked open the front passenger door. "I know he's dead," I said. "Isn't that enough?" I slammed the door behind me. I could feel both detectives watching me as we pulled away, but I kept my eyes forward.

Yeah, I was stone cold. On the outside. But in fact I

was badly shaken. Only days before it had sounded as though things were exactly as Vee had said they would be. Now it sounded like the police knew just about everything.

I got angry. Vee had done this before! Why hadn't she told me? How would I have handled it if she had? Badly. Very badly. Like I said, I'm not one for physical altercations, believe me, I'm not. But she still should have told me. Of course the police would put two and two together with something like that in her past. I thought Vee was too smart to make such an obvious mistake. But she had. She'd used the same ploy twice, and now they were on to her for it.

And then it hit me. They were on to *her* for it. They thought *she*'d done it. For all of Dobrygowski's innuendo, they had only asked about her. Because if they'd asked at the hotel, they'd know that I'd come back that night before the fire could have started. Because I had. And if the deskman told them that, he'd probably also told them that Vee had gone out. She'd had a car brought up from the garage. The garage people would remember that, too, that time of night. If the police thought Vee had done it, well, then part of her plan had worked. The important part. The part about me.

But probably it was just a matter of time until they stumbled upon me. And when they did, I was going to be arrested. And thinking more on it, I was pretty certain they had the death penalty in Maryland. Sure they did. I was going to die here, and there went all of the Rosenkrantzes in one fell swoop. No, not all. Clotilde in her clinic out west was one more. What would become of her?

I had to warn Vee. The way they'd get me for sure was if they got her. She'd spill everything, especially if she thought it might save her.

At Great Aunt Alice's I went right up to my room. I called the Somerset. The front desk answered after only one ring. "Somerset Hotel. How may I assist you?"

"I'd like to reach a party in Suite 12-2," I said. For some reason I knew that I shouldn't ask for Vee by name.

"Of course, sir."

There was a dead click, and then the phone was ringing. "Hello?"

It was a man's voice. I couldn't tell if it was Browne's or someone else's. My tongue was frozen. If it was Browne, the last thing Vee needed was for him to know I was calling. I hung up the phone without saying anything.

I lay back on the bed and tried to think it through, only my mind was caught on a loop thinking the same thing over and over. Vee needed to be moving, she needed to get out of Calvert, and she needed to get as far away as she could, because with that other incident in her past where she'd used arson to cover up murder, there was no way that they wouldn't try to hang Joe's death on her now. How could she be so stupid to use the same scheme? She needed to get out of Calvert. I needed to get through to her, and she needed to get moving. How could she be so stupid?

When it got where I couldn't stand it anymore, I tried the hotel again. Twice. And each time the desk would put me through to Browne's suite and a man would answer the phone and I'd hang up and start my worrying all over.

After the third call, I decided that a whole bunch of hang-ups would be just as bad for Vee as if I were to say who was calling so I resigned myself to waiting until I saw her at our rendezvous the next day. And my thoughts circled and circled all night.

18.

The next day was overcast. Thick ash clouds blocked the sun, but they didn't do one thing to help with the heat. Instead they just trapped the humidity, making the day heavy and draining. I walked from Great Aunt Alice's and arrived at the Somerset ahead of our meeting with a sheen of sweat covering my whole body, my shirt stuck to my back. I took out my handkerchief and wiped my brow and the back of my neck and put it away. My nerves were as frayed as they could be, thinking on it all night, and the only thing that kept me from ducking into the bar for a drink was my heartburn, so bad I thought I might throw up.

Since I was early, I went to the desk to check if I had any messages. I'd asked for them to be forwarded to Great Aunt Alice's—that's how the police had found me last week—but I thought it was odd that I hadn't gotten any messages from *anybody*. I didn't recognize the man at the desk. They had an awful lot of people working there.

"I just checked out about a week ago," I said. "I was wondering if I had any messages that might not have reached me. My name's Shem Rosenkrantz. I was in room 514."

"One moment, sir," the deskman said with no change

of expression. Then he turned and went through a door behind the counter.

I looked around nervously. Did the police have the lobby under surveillance? We probably didn't rate that much attention. They had more important things to do than wait around for some woman who *might* have been involved in a death years earlier that *might* have been a murder. It was just my guilty conscience. But I felt exposed and I worried that I was making a mistake even if I didn't know what it was. At least checking my messages gave me a legitimate reason to be at the hotel.

The deskman came back, and said simply, "No messages, sir."

"No telegrams even?"

"I'm sorry, sir," he said.

No phone calls. No telegrams. I wouldn't need the money now that I had come into the Hadley estate, but still, the idea that my people in New York had forgotten me... All the work we'd done together over the years, all the books we'd published—and I had made them some money, my books had sold pretty well for a few years in there—the idea that a desperate telegram no longer elicited even a response, even a no. I had expected a no, but nothing...

I nodded, and forced a grin, though it didn't feel like it fit my face just then. "Well, thanks," I said.

"Of, course, sir."

I turned back to the lobby, and as I did, Browne went by with two other men in suits. They were intent on the door and didn't see me, but my heart rate jumped so fast

I felt lightheaded. Browne scared me back into child-hood. I was a killer now too, I reminded myself; so what if it had been an accident, with the police and my "motive," it had almost gotten to the point where that didn't matter, the whole thing confused in my mind the way it was. But with all that, I certainly didn't feel like any killer watching the gangster and his bodyguards stroll out of the hotel.

I swallowed and forced myself to move. I didn't want to give the deskman an extra reason to remember me, and standing around like a halfwit was exactly the kind of thing that might get remembered if someone made a point of asking. I started for the luncheonette, but after only a handful of steps it struck me, if Browne had gone out, that meant Vee would be alone on the twelfth floor. We could meet in Browne's suite, and that would be much better than meeting downstairs where anyone could see us and remember the two of us together. I hurried to the elevator, praying that we wouldn't miss each other as I went up to twelve and she went down to the lobby. I pushed the call button, and waited, watching the dial run down the numbers until it reached one, and a bell rang, then rang two more times in quick succession, and then the elevator door slid open.

A slender young mother ushered two children—a boy with Air Force insignia pins on his shirt and a girl in a dress with a bow—out into the lobby. Why had Clotilde and I never had any kids? She would have been such a beautiful mother. And now my only son...

I got in the elevator, and tried once again to organize my thoughts, how the police were onto her and she needed to get out of town. I jiggled with nervous energy, and when the elevator door opened on twelve, I practically ran to Suite 12-2. I knocked at the door, looking along the hallway, hoping to get inside before anyone else went by. When I heard no movement inside, I pounded with a closed fist, painfully aware of the sound traveling.

At last the door jerked open, Vee already saying, "What's the idea—" She was dressed in what was a modest dress for Vee. The bruise on her face had faded to a piebald mess of greens, yellows, purples, and blues. She registered that it was me and said, "Jesus H. Christmas, Shem, what the hell's the matter with you? I said downstairs."

"I saw Browne leave and thought it would be better if we met up here out of sight." I pushed her back into the room and closed the door behind me. "We've got trouble."

" 'We've' got trouble? Ha!" She turned her back on me and stalked across the room. "*I'm* the one living like a prisoner." And she disappeared into the master bedroom. From there, she called, "What's this trouble, you bastard?"

I took a step towards the bedroom, and stopped. The sight of the place hit me hard, almost as if I had only just seen Browne beating on Vee, and my mouth went dry.

"Hello? Idiot! Back here!"

I followed her voice back to the bedroom. She was sitting on the edge of the bed, reaching down to sling a pair of black-and-white heels over her stockinged feet.

"This is the last time I let you pimp me out to a gangster. You nearly got me killed the other night, you know that?"

"Will you lay off of me on that. I'm not a pimp."

She ignored that. "Did you talk to the lawyer yet? You find out when you'll be getting that money? Then I can get out of here."

How had this conversation gotten away from me? I was there for a reason. "You need to go now," I said, but it came out weak.

"And wait for you like a fool, just hoping you show up with the money? Right." She stood up and went over to the bureau, where she picked up a silver pendant earring and cocked her head to put it on.

"Vee, the police…"

She paused, her head still turned to the side. "What about the police?" Her features grew pinched, and if I didn't know before, I knew right then that I could not let Vee hang around and get caught under any circumstances. Because even if right now the police genuinely thought that Vee had acted alone, once they had her in custody she'd be quick to set them straight about that. Hell, she'd probably have a way of putting me in the hot seat without her in it at all. She'd show that broken face of hers and say that I had done that to her if she didn't go and clean up Joe's body. That's exactly what she'd say, and then I'd be right back in it, on my way to death row. If she left, I could sit easy waiting for the money while they chased Vee around the country.

"Shem, you tell me what the hell about the police right this instant."

"You need to get out of here. You need to leave right away."

"Shem—"

"Were you married?"

Her eyes narrowed. "What?"

"The police came to Joe's funeral yesterday. They wanted to know where you were. They say you killed and burned your husband."

"My husband?" Her arms had turned to gooseflesh. With just the one earring hanging, her head looked lopsided.

"In Denver. No. Cleveland."

"What else did they say?"

"They know Joe's skull was fractured. They said they aren't sure it was murder, but…"

"But they brought up Cleveland. Paul. That was years ago." She started forward, but stopped, not sure where she was going.

"Did you kill your husband?" I said.

That woke her back up. She grabbed the other earring. "You don't know what he was like, so don't you even start. And what does it matter to you anyway?"

She wasn't saying no, and even though I knew the answer was yes, I began to feel uneasy with the idea of her running, where I wouldn't know where she was, and I'd worry each minute we were apart.

"Paul had no vision," Vee said. She went to the armoire and pulled out a handful of clothes on their hangers and threw them onto the bed. "He was keeping me trapped in that little town, and a girl can only take that for so long, you know? But he just wouldn't listen."

"What are you doing?"

"What am I doing? I'm leaving. I'm getting the hell out of this city. I'm not stupid. If they're talking about Paul, it's because they want to hang your kid on me too, and I'm not getting sent up for something I didn't have anything to do with."

Hearing her say it, that she was going to leave, that she was doing what I wanted her to do, suddenly filled me with an even greater sense of dread.

She dumped more clothing onto the bed and pulled out a suitcase. "You better get out of here. Carlton's supposed to be out all day, but you never know with him."

That threat didn't even stir me. My mind was trying to catch on something. Something I hadn't thought through in the whole night of thinking. "Where will you go?" I said.

"Who cares? Not here."

Yes, 'who cares?' That was Vee. I knew then what I had probably already known. Even if she ran, they would catch her.

She had her bag half packed, and was forcing stuff into it with no regard.

Yeah, they would catch her, because if she ran it would look guilty as anything, and they'd put everything into catching her. "You can't run," I said.

She looked at me and put her hands on her hips. "You're the one who said I should leave."

"I was wrong. I hadn't thought it through. They'll think for sure you did it then, if you run."

"So I'm supposed to wait right where they probably know where I am. That's your brilliant idea."

I was desperate suddenly for a way to keep her from walking out the door. "You can't leave me," I said.

"Oh, Mr. Sentimental. You got my face beat in and then got me tangled up in a murder. I should have left you the day I met you. You'd have thought I'd never been around the block before, starstruck for a has-been writer. All because one of your books made me cry as a girl."

"I got the money."

That stopped her. She did want that money. "What do you mean you got the money?"

"I got the money. I'm getting it. The whole two million, it's mine. Now that Joe's dead." I knew she wouldn't be able to resist the money, just like I knew they'd catch her when she ran, and she'd pull me into it.

"You're sure?"

I nodded.

She blinked rapidly, and shook her head. "How long till you get it?" She spoke deliberately, as though she was afraid I might skitter away if she talked too suddenly.

"I don't know. I'm meeting with the lawyer soon. Today maybe. These things take time. Maybe a week or two. Certainly by the end of the month."

"The end of the month!"

"It'll be sooner than that." I had no idea how long it would be, but as badly as I needed her to run before, I needed to keep her there with me now.

Her face was dead serious as she looked at me across the clothing-strewn bed. "I want us to get married," she said.

I almost laughed at that one. Married! I couldn't even

believe she'd been married before I knew her. And she killed that guy. "I can't. I'm still married to Clotilde."

"You can get a divorce. She's in the loony bin."

I shook my head. "I'm not getting a divorce."

"Well, something. I need to know that I'll get my cut of what's coming."

"You'll get your cut," I said. I saw in her eyes that I had her hooked. I'd be able to keep her where I could watch her. Having killed Joe was already nearly killing me, my whole chest on fire from reflux, but I wasn't going to sit in any electric chair.

"Fifty-fifty."

"We'll see."

"Fifty-fifty," she said again. "It's my neck hanging out there."

I saw then what you probably saw at the start. They'd get her if she stayed or if she left.

"Sure. Of course," I said. "That's fair."

She searched my face, still wary. "You know what I'd do to you if you cross me."

"I'd never cross you."

She was reluctant, but she must have decided that was the best she was going to get right then. She started putting clothing back into the armoire. I watched her do it, and I was suddenly more exhausted than I'd ever been in my life. Exhausted because there was only one way I would know she wouldn't talk, and being in the room with her after thinking that, well, it just got real hard. Carrying my body around seemed like a horrible inconvenience. My head was falling off my neck and my eyelids were like quarters over my eyes. I wanted to lie down and never get up again. Because I had to kill her, and that was worse even than thinking about how I'd already killed Joe.

"I'm so tired," I said.

She went around the bed and sat down at the vanity. "So get out. Go home, sleep."

I could tell by the way she said it that she was still awfully unsettled by the fact that the police were asking about her and bringing up what she thought was ancient history. If her nerves could be rattled so easily... Killing her really was my only choice.

"It's going to be all right," I said.

"I know that," she said. "I'm probably safer with Carlton than anywhere else anyway. The cops wouldn't touch one of Carlton's girls." She folded a tissue, put it between her lips, and closed her mouth quickly and opened it, blotting her lipstick.

As she talked I felt heavier and heavier. Could Browne really protect her from a murder charge? And what about protecting her from him? He'd attacked her at the sight of me. I had a feeling he wouldn't take it too kindly if he knew where she had gone afterwards, what she had done with me. Men like Carlton Browne don't let any of the dirty work get anywhere near them, so they always have deniability, and this was right up next to him.

Vee finished her makeup, stood, and turned to me. "Well, how do I look?" The bruise was still visible, but it wasn't as pronounced. Even with the puffiness on that side of her face, she looked like a million bucks. She knew what she had, and she knew how to use it.

"Like a killer," I said.

She laughed, a big open-mouthed laugh, throwing her head back to really get it out there. "Come here. Let me give you a present." I didn't move, and she pouted a little, but then she came over to me. She gave me a kiss on the cheek. It made me think that there was no way I'd ever be able to go through with it.

Then, with her mouth right near my ear. "Who was that girl you were with the other day?"

I looked at her, incredulous, and I knew I'd be able to kill her after all. "You're all dolled up for some other man, and you're going to be jealous?"

Her face turned mean again. "That's work, and you know it. Carlton expects me to be on call."

"That was Joe's fiancée," I said.

Her expression softened. "Is that why her face was all runny? Oh little girl, you've got a lot to learn." And she laughed her ugly laugh again, and I could have killed her right then if I knew how to do it without putting me in it.

"I better go," I said.

"We ought to celebrate," she said.

"Celebrate?"

"The money," she said. "We can have a lunch in the dining room. I think that's safe enough, don't you?"

"I don't know."

"Yes, it is. Just give me a couple of hours to get myself together. I need to, I don't know, untwist my mind. Two million dollars! Sweet Mary! I always knew I deserved this." And she kissed me again and then that horrible laugh. It made my stomach turn over. "Ha! Two million dollars. My luck's really changing now."

"Yeah, sure," I said, thinking, if only she knew. "Noon, we'll say. Downstairs. I'm going now."

"Wait," she said, and she stepped forward, and wiped some lipstick from my cheek. It was such a gentle gesture, and it made me sick. Because sure I'd killed Joe, but that was an accident. And this… This wouldn't be.

She stepped back. "Okay," she said.

But nothing was okay. Nothing.

19.

The thing about killing is... You see, when you've decided to kill someone... What am I trying to say? I think I mentioned that Joe wasn't the first person I'd seen who'd met a violent end. I had a girlfriend, a girl I knew, back when I could get a little work in Hollywood, even if it was only because Clotilde pulled some strings. This girl, she was a waitress at a nightclub with aspirations to Hollywood stardom. What I'm saying is that she was one of thousands of girls out in S.A. who all are waiting for their moment to come, convinced they'll be discovered, that someone on the street will stop them, and say, 'You oughta be in pictures.' Yeah, this girl was just a dime a dozen, but I'd met her, and I started seeing her, and I even got her cast in one of Clotilde's pictures. I've always been a real upstanding guy, huh?

Clotilde was starting to have more and more trouble with her nerves, jumping at shadows, playing the wronged woman, convinced that a slew of people were out to get her, including me. It didn't matter that I actually *was* stepping out with this other girl, the point is, I'd never have done anything to hurt Clotilde. I mean it. She was always the joy of my life, the one thing that mattered, and if I was going out with this other girl, it was only because I couldn't help it, I just needed something Clotilde couldn't give me, suffering the way she was.

Now that I think of it, that was about the time I started borrowing money from Hub Gilplaine. He owned the nightclub where I met this girl, and we were friends... Gee, it's funny how the pattern of your life gets stitched from all these different threads, none of which seem important at the time, just day-to-day living, and then someone starts worrying one of those threads, just gives it a little pull, and your whole life starts to unravel. But maybe it was before that even, back when Quinn and I were still married...

Anyway, I went over to this waitress' house in San Angelo, late one night, and I let myself in with my key, and I went into her bedroom, and there she was, all cut up and blood everywhere. It was a thousand times worse than what happened to Joe. I shriveled up then. Anyone would have, even the toughest cold-blooded murderer on death row. And I was just an effete writer who told himself he was hardboiled but really wasn't anything but a husk of a man, if that.

So I've seen the worst, and the only thing that made Joe as bad as all that was that I did it myself. Now I was planning to do it for real, on purpose, and it just about was all I could do to make myself think about it. Because if you thought too much about it, how a person was a body, just a biological machine that was, honestly, quite easy to break, but a person was also so much more, the stuff that all of the world's religions and artists and writers had spent all of human existence trying to understand... Well, you see where your mind starts to go. It had been that way for a long time after my girlfriend got cut up with me trying to understand what and why. And now it was like that in thinking about Vee, and what I needed to do. I had to kill her. It was the only way I'd be safe. But my mind kept slipping back to that cut-up girl in S.A., and I couldn't think straight, even if I knew I *had* to think it out or I'd end up in a jam over Vee's death too.

Well, there's no surprise that I was doing all of this thinking in the hotel bar, but I was tossing back far fewer than you would have thought. I was hardly even buzzed. I played out different scenarios. Getting Vee out of the hotel into a bad part of the city and making it look like a mugging. Only that was just improbable enough that the police would probably know she'd been killed to shut her up. Throwing her down the stairs. But why hadn't she used the elevator? Any good cop would find that too suspicious. I didn't know anything about poisons, didn't know much more about weapons. And it needed to look like an accident.

It didn't help that with each plot, the blood from that long-ago night in S.A. kept trying to drown out all of my thoughts. The only reason I hadn't been a suspect then was because I had a good alibi. Even if I could orchestrate a good alibi for Vee's death, it still might seem convenient enough to reinvigorate the investigation into Joe's death, which left me at risk. The police had to be certain that Joe had been murdered by Vee. These ideas twisted and curled in my mind, spiraling out questions that hit brick walls, banging up against them again and again, as I tried in vain to find an answer, increasingly anxious that I didn't have one.

And that was a familiar feeling. The steady flow of ideas discarded one by one, with each failure constricting me further and further in inaction. That was writing. Killing someone was a whole lot like writing, a creative endeavor. I was trying to manipulate characters to do what I wanted them to do while trying to figure out how it would all play out afterwards to get the effect I wanted. I was anxious, but a part of me enjoyed what I was doing. And with that realization, a door opened up in my mind to show me new space—it didn't have to be an accident if it was suicide.

But Healey and Dobrygowski thought she'd done it for the money. Why would she then kill herself? Maybe if she knew they were on to her, especially if they brought up that old husband case. It had really given her pause when I told her about that. Yeah, she found out they were on to her, and she killed herself.

Well, by the time I had it worked out that far, it was almost noon and I had to meet Vee for lunch in the main dining room. I didn't like that we'd be so exposed, but I couldn't do anything that would arouse her suspicion, and skipping our celebratory lunch would have done just that. Before I left, I put my plan into action. If I was going to do it, I ought to do it. I asked the bartender for a phone. He brought it to me, and retreated discreetly.

I had the operator put me through to the *Sun*. "Taylor Montgomery please." The switchboard did whatever it does, and Montgomery answered in a voice that sounded much gruffer than in person. "Montgomery here."

"Taylor, son, it's Shem Rosenkrantz."

His voice softened into the fawning young man I knew. "Mr. Rosenkrantz! What can I do for you?"

"Would the paper be interested in running a follow-up

on Joe's death? The police think it was a murder now."

"Oh no, that's horrible," he said, genuinely pained.

I made sure to increase the sorrow in my own voice, although it was probably unnecessary. "They think this woman I know, Victoria Abrams, did it. She apparently did the same thing in Cleveland a while back under a different name. Killed her husband and burned the house down."

"Abrams, you said?" He was writing it down.

"Victoria Abrams." If the police found out I'd made this call, planting the story would look bad for me, so I made my intentions very clear. "If this woman did this thing, I want her nailed for it, and I don't trust the police to carry it through. But if the *Sun* runs a story about it, maybe something'll actually get done."

"Of course, of course," Montgomery said, his voice somewhat muffled, so I knew he was holding the receiver with his shoulder, using both hands to write or check a file or something.

"Will they let you run it? It's not big news, I know."

"They'll run it. You're still a celebrity and the Hadleys are a big deal in this town, even if they are on the way down. I mean—"

"No offense taken."

"I'll make sure they run it."

"Good. And check on this thing in Cleveland."

"As soon as we hang up the phone," he said.

"That a boy." And we rang off. I knew he'd do all that he could to get it on page one of the city section. And it would be thorough and it would be damning and I would be an innocent victim, and me a great man. And if Vee was guilty in the paper, it hardly mattered if she was guilty or not, the police would have to do something. At least, that's what Vee would think. And that's why she was going to kill herself. A stretch, but a plan. I felt the high of a good writing session, the same energy and self-assurance, as I left the bar to cross the hotel lobby.

We arrived at the dining room at exactly the same time. She'd changed again, now wearing a royal blue tea dress with an oversized white belt cinched around her waist, an outfit I'd never seen before that was no doubt a gift from Browne. She tried to look demure, biting her lip to keep from smiling and failing. All her teeth came out in a huge sappy grin. She moved towards me, but then checked herself. She might have thrown Browne over in her head, but she couldn't be seen getting too familiar with another man just yet. I felt the same way, my confidence waning, worried that the police had their eyes on us right then.

"Mr. Rosenkrantz," Vee said.

"You look stunning, Vee," I said.

She actually hung her head at the compliment. "I'm glad you think so," she said, and then stepped forward and took my arm. "Well, I guess I can be escorted by a gentleman friend without anyone thinking anything of it."

Despite her hanging on me like that, I was surprised to find that I didn't actually feel anything about what I planned to do to her later. It was as though that part of me was closed off, protected from what I was doing right then. I led her into the dining room.

They sat us at a four-person table in the center of the room. The lighting from the chandeliers was just enough to see by, augmented by a shaded candlestick in the center of the table, which cast a flickering circle on the tablecloth. A good number of tables were filled with hotel guests and maybe some locals there for the cuisine. Tuxedoed waiters moved quickly between the tables. Jacketless Negro food runners and busboys carried platters at shoulder height.

I held the chair for her like we were two regular people, and then sat across from her. She leaned forward, and the candle lit her face from below as though she were telling a ghost story at a campfire. "We're gonna eat at places like this all the time," she said, "and I won't have to sleep with any more gangsters to do it. We're coming up in the world finally."

"I've been up in the world. This is still coming down for me."

She crunched her face into a pout. "Well, excuse me, Mr. Big-Time New York Writer. Not all of us had movie star wives and vacationed on the Riviera."

I shouldn't have done that to her, taken the air out of her balloon. She had a right to be happy for a little while. But I felt like being mean for some reason. I said, "*Have* a movie star wife. I'm still married to her."

Her face turned into that familiar hard-boiled stare, and she said, "I'm your woman now, you got that? I don't want to hear about any wife or anybody. We're in this thing together. That money's mine just as much as it is yours."

"Oh, just the two of us? But I know you're always for hire. If we're each other's one and only, how are you going to ditch your boyfriend?"

"You pimp—" she started, but she saw where this was going, and she visibly stopped, closed her eyes and took a deep breath. "Let's just forget all of that," she said. "This is a chance for us to start again."

Seeing her try so hard like that really made me feel like scum, and I said, "Of course. You're right." I reached across the table and gave her hand a squeeze.

Her expression softened, and soon she was smiling. She laughed to herself, and I knew she was thinking about all that money that was hers.

I grabbed a passing waiter and ordered a Gin Rickey. Vee asked for a Manhattan. Then we both fell silent over our menus. And the whole thing felt perfectly natural. We were a wealthy couple enjoying a wealthy meal in a wealthy hotel. It's true that there was a time in my life when that was a regular occurrence, but just then, I couldn't help but feel as though we were playacting. And that started me wondering if I was playacting at the other thing also, but…I couldn't think about that right then. I couldn't risk Vee thinking something was up.

And then suddenly, a loud voice cut through the room from the doorway, and I turned to see Carlton Browne striding for our table.

20.

He came at us, with the maître d' following him.

"Would you look at that," Browne said. "It's your cousin, Vee." He emphasized the word 'cousin' as though it were a shared password that should be taken to mean something else. He came right up to me and gripped me around the arm where Joe's ice pick had sliced me. The pain shot through my arm. I sucked in and held my breath as my stomach turned. "This really is a small hotel, huh? How you doing?" He ground his fingers into my bicep leaving no doubt that he knew exactly what he was doing.

He looked at the maître d', who was standing a few steps back, his hands out and his mouth open as though he were trying to catch something delicate. "I'll join this table. How about a bottle of red and a bottle of white? And a Scotch for me. Anyone else?" He looked between Vee and me, then turned to the maître d'. "A Scotch for both the men." He released my arm, and I let out my breath.

"We've already ordered drinks," Vee said.

"Good. So you'll have some more." He took the chair to my right with Vee on his right. "You don't mind. The lady and I like to sit together."

Vee kept her eyes on the tablecloth, her hands fidgeting with the napkin in her lap.

I did what I could to avoid looking at Browne, which

wasn't much. He was younger than I had thought, no more than forty, probably younger. He was balding, his hairline eroded in two fierce arches from his forehead back to the top of his head. He was big in every way, tall, muscular, and fat, if you can imagine that.

Our drinks came, and I took half of mine in one gulp.

"It's funny us all being here like this," Browne said. He seemed to revel in our discomfort. "Huh, Vee?" He gave her a playful tap on the chin with a closed fist, but the intent was far from playful, carrying what it did behind it. "Sorry, what was your name?" he said, turning to me. "I was a little distracted the other night, I'm not sure I got it."

"Shem Rosenkrantz," I said.

He frowned. "That's a Jew name, isn't it? Vee, I didn't know you were a Jew."

"I'm not," Vee said, leading with her whole body. "You see—"

He raised a hand, silencing her without even looking at her. "Sure, sure. It's not important. We're all white. What's it matter? Still, I'd like to have known you were a Jew, Vee. You should have told me that."

Vee looked at her hands in her lap. A small ring of silence had fallen at the tables around us, like Browne sucked all of the energy out of his surroundings.

"So how are you related? I'm still not clear on that," Browne said.

"Carlton—" Vee started.

He sneered at her. "I wasn't asking you. Was I asking you?" She said nothing, her head down, chastised. "You'd think you could knock some sense into her, huh?" He grabbed her bicep as he had grabbed mine, and Vee's face turned sour, and she looked away from him. I had never seen her so cowed, and it frightened me even more than Browne's patter. When the maître d' set down our Scotches, and then turned to a busboy behind him holding the bottles of wine, I picked up my Gin Rickey and drank the rest of it down.

"Shem Rosenkrantz..." Browne said, ignoring the wait staff and still holding Vee by the arm. "Oh, wait, did I read something in the paper about your son getting killed?"

"My son died, yes," I said. "But he wasn't killed."

"Oh, sure. I read the paper," and he gave me an exaggerated frown. "But I get the real news, too. Outside the paper. He was killed and someone tried to burn his body."

I tried to tell if he was just talking or if he knew something. It made me nervous, and as I shifted in my seat, I tried to catch Vee's eye to see if she had told him, but she was sitting with her eyes down like a kid in trouble with her folks.

Browne leaned back, and grabbed a passing busboy by the sleeve. "I want to order," he said.

"I'll find your waiter, sir," the busboy said.

"I don't want you to find my waiter. I want you to tell him. Whatever's not on the menu, that's what we want. All around." He spun his finger to indicate the whole table.

"Yes, sir," the busboy said, nodding more than he needed to.

"Ha. 'Sir.' And they say kids aren't learning any manners these days. You're smart, kid, you'll go far if you keep that up." He released the boy, who hurried back in the direction of the kitchen.

Browne grabbed a bottle of wine, and poured Vee a glass before filling his own. "That's tough about your son," he said to me. He shook his head. "Nothing's more important than family. I've got three little angels myself, and they're my whole world. Ask Vee, she'll tell you. I talk about 'em all the time, don't I?" He waited. "Don't I?"

"He does," Vee said, as though she needed to plead his case to me.

"You see that. I talk about 'em all the time, because there's nothing more important than family. Isn't that right, Rosy?"

I exhaled through my nose.

"Yeah, you're in mourning. I see that. If anything happened to my kids, I'd kill the bastard who did it. I mean with my own hands, right here, I'd kill him."

The comment made me think about how all three of us at the table had killed someone at some point, and I was planning to do it again. This was what my life had become.

I drank, while Browne stared at me intently. I was supposed to speak. "I feel like my life is over," I said, and I really did. I'd probably have been happy if Browne'd stood up and shot me right there. Not that he'd ever do that, he was too cagey for that. That's why he could sit out in public like this, like a respected citizen, because he was a respected citizen. Nothing ever stuck to him.

"You always feel like that," Vee said, deciding that the

best course of action was to ridicule me, which she had a lot of practice doing despite our newfound camaraderie.

"Hey," Browne snapped. "He's in mourning."

"But he does. He whines about everything—"

"If you don't shut it," Browne said, "I'm gonna shut it for you." He brandished his fist. Then turning to me: "You tell me about your son. I want to hear. It'll be good for you to talk. I've learned that the hard way. You can't keep it all pent up inside you. Go on, tell me."

I looked at Vee. She looked like she was going to throw up at any moment. She crossed her arms, and rubbed as though she were cold.

"What can I say? I never really knew Joe," I said.

Browne was nodding with deep understanding.

"He lived with his mother all his life. I wasn't even there when he was born. I think he was maybe two when I saw him the first time. It seems stupid now. Stupid that I didn't know him. But I guess I would say that my parents didn't know me, and I grew up right in the same house with them. They could never understand my love of books. But they read everything I wrote and were proud of me, even if they didn't understand them."

"You're a writer, huh? What do you write?"

"Novels. Movies."

"What movies?"

I shook my head and shrugged.

He didn't seem to care that I didn't have an answer. "My mother lives with us now," he said. "You got to keep the whole family together, tight." He reached over and patted Vee on the cheek. The gesture was to show owner-ship. "You don't even have a mother, do you, Vee? Nah, no mother'd let her baby be like you." He looked back at me. "You can't even imagine loving somebody until you have a kid. You can hardly love a woman," he said. "Maybe your brother. It's family, always family." He looked me straight in the eye. "We never know what we've got when we've got it, and we always kill what means the most to us, huh?"

I still couldn't tell if he knew, if Vee had told him. He seemed to be needling me purposely, going on about family, making the remarks about killing, like he really wanted to get to me, to see if I'd crack. Was it possible that he was afraid of being caught up in the murder if it went the wrong way? Nah, he couldn't worry about that in this town. Nothing would come near him. He wanted to tear me down because I had violated his space, and it was certain he knew about Vee's and my true relationship.

The food was brought over, a team of three men, two carrying plates, and the chef himself standing next to Mr. Browne with his hands clenched together. He went through a detailed description of what was being served, but I didn't hear any of it, and I don't think Browne or Vee did either. When the serving team had left, Browne dug right in. Apparently there was no talking while eating, and since Browne had fallen silent, neither of us was going to make any attempt at small talk.

I finished my Scotch and had several glasses of wine too. As Browne was wiping up his plate with a piece of bread he said in a quiet, measured voice, "Rosy. You're sleeping with my mistress and you've been living the high life on my dime." Vee and I froze. "I could have you killed tonight if I wanted to, but you've already taken a pretty bad blow, and you're set to take another at any moment."

I knew then that he knew, and I knew my life was over.

"You know," he said, and took a gulp of wine, "you and I have a mutual friend."

My stomach boiled. I could feel it in the back of my throat.

"Great guy, out in S.A."

I knew what he was going to say before he said it, and now I knew who had bought up my debt.

"Hub Gilplaine," he said.

I felt my face grow slack.

He took another gulp of wine, nodding to indicate he was still going to say something. "Vee tells me that you just came into some money. She said something about two million dollars."

He paused for me to say something, but I couldn't even swallow, my mouth was so dry.

"Now, really, I don't care who Vee sleeps with, I'd be crazy if I did. If it was my wife, I'd kill you both, but Vee, she's not wife material. She just needs to know who's boss. And you know who, right, honey?"

Vee looked like she might cry. I'd never seen her like that. She was the strongest, loudest, most demanding woman I'd ever met, and I'd met a lot of loud women. But I knew now that she could be beaten, in both the literal and metaphorical sense, and that my concern over her setting me up for a fall should she take a tumble was absolutely correct. Yes, she had to die. That Browne had gotten it out of her was trouble enough. Now neither of us was going to see any of that money.

"I've got a wife too," I said.

"Good for you. Remind me to send her a present."

"She's sick. She needs to stay in the hospital. It's very expensive."

"I'm crying on the inside."

"Please." I thought about all his talk about family. "She's the only family I've got left," I tried.

"We'll take that into consideration," he said. "Now, you owe me five hundred thousand dollars."

"But I only owed fifteen grand to Hub," I said, and could hear I was whining.

"Let me explain to you how this works," Browne said. "When someone buys up your debt, it's like refinancing your house. The deal changes. And you owe me five hundred thousand dollars."

I didn't say anything.

He stood. "I'll give you a little time for the estate to come through, but if I don't get my money on that day, it goes up by five grand a day until I get it, because you're gonna have the dough." He stood, and put his hand on the back of Vee's neck. "That leaves you some for your wife's hospital bills, right?" Vee winced, and I knew he had tightened his fist. "You didn't think you were getting any of that money, did you, Vee?"

She looked across at me, and her eyes were shiny with tears. "No."

"Of course not," he said. She winced again. "There's something I've got to go see about. You'll be in the room when I get back." It was an order. "Here's the key." He dropped it beside her, and I remembered I still had the other key to the room. Either he didn't remember or he didn't care about getting it back. Instead, he looked at me, and said, "Stay. Enjoy some coffee. Dessert. It's all on me. I think it's going to be nice doing business with you, Rosy." He raised his voice. "Excellent as always," he said to no one in particular, and he wove his way through the tables and out the door.

The two of us sat in silence. It was as though I'd been hit by a truck. I was so despondent I wished I actually *had* been hit by a truck. I thought about going out into the street to see if it could be arranged. *Wham!* Goodbye troubles.

At last, Vee stood up, threw her napkin on the table, and walked out without a word.

I just kept sitting, looking at nothing, and wishing I were dead.

21.

I sat there a long time. It wasn't until the third time the waiter came around to offer me coffee that I could look him in the eye when I shook my head no.

But that wasn't good enough for him. He was a real sentimentalist. "Are you all right, sir?"

I couldn't do more than press my lips together and shrug over and over, exposing my palms again and again: I don't know, I don't know. I was on the verge of tears.

"Take your time." And he stepped away.

My mind circled. I needed to get out of Calvert. Healey and Dobrygowski wouldn't like it, it would look suspicious, but I wasn't going to risk any more time in the city than I needed to. Browne could get at me too easily if I stayed. Five hundred thousand dollars! What was I going to do? Palmer had said I was getting some money from the estate, but I certainly didn't know if it was going to be that much. Sure, it was *supposed* to be two million, but it wasn't in the bank yet. And the will might still be contested, and there would be legal fees... How could Hub do this to me? I was going to pay him back! We were supposed to be friends. And just like that, my fear turned to rage—I wanted to kill Hub. I wanted to kill Browne, and Vee, and everyone else. I wanted to kill them all.

But I couldn't think like that. It was thinking like that

that would get me all fouled up. I'd had too much to drink with lunch. I needed to get straight.

I looked around. Most of the lunch crowd had left, and busboys were clearing tables into a bin on a rolling cart. My waiter hovered a few tables away, watching me. I gave a weak smile and nod, pulled myself together, and got up to leave.

In the lobby, I stood halfway between the elevator bank and the front entrance, unsure where to go and what to do. My anger had drained off, leaving me exhausted, and now there was only one thought running through my head: I needed to get out of town if I wanted to live.

But what about Vee? I couldn't trust Vee. And I couldn't bring her with me. That would look far too suspicious. I thought of my original plan, before this lunch fiasco, the decision I'd made with a clear head, not out of anger. For peace of mind, to at least neutralize the risk of the police, Vee had to die. If there had been any doubt before, I didn't have the luxury to entertain it now. Now it needed to happen and fast. Tonight. And I needed to figure the way to do it.

That's what I was thinking as I stood there, working out again why Vee needed to die, when all of a sudden I got the feeling that I was being watched. I hated that feeling. It reminded me of Clotilde's paranoia, and it always made me worry about my own mental health. But I just couldn't shake it. So I scanned the lobby, and zeroed in on a man sitting in one of the overstuffed easy chairs across from the front desk. He wore a tailored suit and had one foot resting on the opposite knee, with a paper spread out before him on his lap. I watched him, and I was certain that his eyes kept darting up from the paper, focusing on me. Did the police have me under surveillance? That would be bad. That would be very bad.

I turned suddenly and went out the revolving doors, and hurried across the street into the First Calvert City Bank. It was a large edifice, the ceiling rising three stories above with two exposed balconies hanging over the tellers. A line of people, men and women, stood watching the "Next Teller" sign light and ring and following its command like Pavlov's dogs. I turned my back on them, and stepped over to a chest-high counter that ran along the front windows, where I pretended to make out a withdrawal slip. I kept my eyes on the hotel's entrance, waiting for the man I had seen to come out after me, expecting him any moment.

I waited long enough to fill out the withdrawal slip ten times, but he never appeared, nor did anyone else who seemed on the lookout for where I had gone. This worried me almost as much as if he had followed me. Maybe I really was going crazy like Clotilde. People who decide to kill other people aren't sane, right? But thinking like that wasn't going to get done what needed to get done. So I pushed it away into the same corner of my head where I'd hidden Joe's death as best as possible, and made a pact with myself to wait another five minutes, measuring them on my watch.

After three minutes no one had appeared and I'd had enough. I left the bank and began to wander the streets with no clear plan, but heading uptown towards Great Aunt Alice's all the same. Halfway there it occurred to me, if the man at the Somerset wasn't a cop, maybe he was one of Browne's men. I tried to place him as one of the men I'd seen walking out with Browne that morning, but my mental image of them was almost nonexistent. Browne had been alone when he came into the dining room, and he'd been alone the night I'd…visited him. So it was just as likely that he didn't have men with him all of the time. And I didn't even know for sure that the man in the lobby had been looking at me.

My thoughts chased one another like that, and I traversed the blocks without seeing the city around me. I was lost again in the same way I got when writing. I could thank Taylor Montgomery for that. He had reawakened my creative impulse after it had remained unexercised so long, and now I was putting it to good use. In a way, he was responsible for my new career as a criminal. He was even setting Vee up for me with the article in tonight's evening paper. That made him practically an accomplice. I started to feel guilty about leaving him, what with how important my interest in his writing was to him. A blow to a writer's optimism like that could set him back years. I promised myself I'd write him a letter before I left. If I left…if I…no, when I left. After I'd done this one last difficult thing.

I got to Great Aunt Alice's then. Connie let me in. Her expression at the sight of me was one of heavy concern. I must have looked worse than I knew, and I wondered if it was my fear or my new grim conviction that showed. It could have just been the day's liquor.

"Will you be to dinner tonight, Mr. Shem?" she asked.

"I can't say that I know," I said.

"Mrs. Hadley is wanting to see you and she was hoping you would be to dinner."

Great Aunt Alice. I couldn't handle Great Aunt Alice on top of everything else just then. But I was staying in her house, eating her food... I bit the bullet. "I could see her now," I said, taking the attitude that the sooner it was started, the sooner it would be over.

"Mrs. Hadley is indisposed for the rest of the afternoon. She really hoped you'd be to dinner."

I tried to smile, but it wasn't in me. "I'll see what I can do," I said, and went upstairs without waiting for another exchange. The last thing I needed was to worry about what Great Aunt Alice and Connie thought of me.

In my room, I retrieved my duffel bag from beneath the bed, and started pulling my clothes out of the closet and stuffing them in without any semblance of order. It couldn't have been more than five minutes before I was packed and ready to go. I stood beside the bed, supporting some of my weight by leaning on the duffel bag with two of my fingers. I stood that way for three or four, oh, I don't know how many minutes, and asked myself again why I couldn't just pick up and leave right then. It was twenty to two.

I picked up the phone with the intention of calling the Enoch White clinic and getting Clotilde on the line. She'd remind me what I was doing this for. Just hearing her voice, the relief and good will she'd had when I told her we'd gotten the money, that would shore up my nerve. But instead of dialing California, I found myself calling Joe's girl Mary.

A maid answered the phone. How come you could

never get anybody just straight? She put the phone down, and I could hear the echoing sounds of her walking away, and then a door closing. There were some loud clanks as the receiver was picked up, and Mary said, "All right, Louise," another clank as the maid set the receiver back into the cradle, and then, "Mr. Rosenkrantz, I'm so glad you called."

I let out my breath, and found that I didn't know what I had intended to say to her. "Mary, I'm so sorry," I said, and it came out as a sob. What was I doing? Was I going to break down and throw it all away? I shook my head, regaining control of my voice. "I'm sorry," I said again.

"No, I'm sorry, Mr. Rosenkrantz. I'm sorry I ran off yesterday after the service. I was so stunned I didn't know what to do." She laughed, but it sounded hollow. "My father even made me drink out of his flask, I was so distraught."

"I saw that," I said, pinching the bridge of my nose with my free hand.

"You did," she said, guilty. "Oh, well, I guess it was all right under the circumstances. That's what my father said."

"Of course. Of course."

"So you weren't angry that I didn't say anything to you."

"I was in shock myself," I said. "If I could do anything about all of this…"

"I've been saying that to myself for a week now," she said in a brave voice.

"The estate—" I started, but she interrupted.

"I don't care about that. It's not about that. It never was."

And that made me feel better. Maybe that's why I had called, to hear her say that, to assuage at least some of my guilt. A fine murderer I was, let me tell you.

"I just wonder if I'll ever stop missing him." She paused. "Did you ever stop missing Quinn? After the divorce, I mean," she said, and hurried to add, "if that's not too bad of me to ask."

"It wasn't the same with Quinn. We hated each other as much as we loved each other."

"Like Joe and you."

That hit me in the gut.

"I'm sorry," she said, realizing what she'd said. "I didn't mean that."

"No, it's okay. It's true. Like me and Joe. Not like what you had at all."

"So you think it won't go away?" she said.

I wondered that myself. Would Joe's death ever go away for me, the clunk of his head, the weight of his body as I carried him up the steps? And soon I planned to add Vee to that. And Browne, flashed into my mind. If I wanted to be certain that enough of Quinn's money went to setting Clotilde up for a very long time, Browne would have to die too. After all, Vee must have told him about the murder when she'd told him about the money. If they both were to die, then no one else would know, and I could walk away from the whole thing free. But not otherwise.

"Mr. Rosenkrantz?" Mary said.

"It'll go away," I said, needing that to be true. "You'll meet someone else. You'll move on. And every now and then you'll wonder, what if?, maybe around the anniversary

of his death, but as you get older, things seem less important." Was that true? I sure as hell didn't know.

"I don't think it'll ever get better," she said, resolute.

"I hope you're wrong," I said.

"But we can still write, can't we? You wouldn't be
mad if I sent you letters. It would be kind of like—" She
broke off.

"Kind of like writing to him."

"Yeah."

And if that didn't make me feel like a heel, then what
would. It had been a mistake calling her. It was a mistake
to expect anybody to be of help then. That's what this was
all about, carrying it on my own.

I realized she was waiting for me to answer. "Sure," I
said. "You can write any time."

"Thank you," she said, and expelled a sigh.

"I better be going now," I said, needing this call to be
over.

"I'm so glad you called. I'm glad that Joe and you had
made it up before he died. At least there was that."

"I'll wait for your letters," I said. I put the receiver
down but left my hand on it. I felt better about the money,
but about a thousand times worse about everything else,
and that was exactly what I didn't need.

My mind ran back to my flash of insight while I was
talking to Mary, that Browne had to die as well. Whether
he knew about the murder or not, he didn't need to have
something on me to blackmail me. He'd kill me if I didn't
pay him, and that was all the motivation he needed to
rely on. Part of me knew somewhere the second he sat
down at lunch with us this afternoon that it would come

down to me killing him or him killing me. That's where all of the fear, the paranoia, was coming from, because for this to work, for me to set up Clotilde and myself, they both had to die...

I took my hand from the receiver. Nothing would be gained by calling Clotilde now. I had to do this alone. I sat down on the bed beside my duffel bag, and let it all sink in. I knew that killing two people, one of whom was bigger than me and much more accustomed to violence, was not going to be at all the same as a lucky push. But what choice did I have? And what did I have to lose? If I waited it out it would come to the same thing in the end, because I wasn't stupid enough to think Browne'd leave it at five hundred thousand dollars when he found out just how much I got. In the end, it would still be them or me.

And I couldn't feel bad for either of them. Browne was a criminal, after all. He knew the risk when he chose his way of life. He probably expected to get killed someday. And Vee? Vee was little better than a whore, and she knew it. If she was going to live by spongeing off of gangsters who beat her, she was playing Russian roulette already anyway.

And then it all fell into place. Browne could come home and beat Vee. Hell, he probably would. Maybe even strangle her. But this time, during the struggle, Vee could manage to get her gun—the gun she kept in her bag, the one he made her carry—she'd get it and shoot him with it. She'd still die, but she'd get him first. Yeah, killing two people could actually make the whole thing much easier, because I could make it look like *they'd* killed each other. And the cops would have an open-and-shut case with one of the biggest criminals in Calvert dead, so no one would be eager to check too closely. They could even pin Joe's death on them if Montgomery's article stirred up any noise about that. It was like a present to the police. And I'd be home free. I just needed to let myself into the suite with my key before Browne got back, beat Vee to death, and then wait for Browne with Vee's gun.

I tried to think of holes in the plan, and it seemed sound any way I looked at it. I didn't think about the fact that I had never hit anyone in my life, let alone a woman. But would I have done anything differently if I had considered it? When you feel the noose tightening around your neck, you don't stop kicking because the movement's pulling the knot tighter. You kick right to the end. Yeah, I would have still done it, kicking all the way.

22.

I had to pass a few hours before I could go back to the hotel. I needed to kill them both within as short a time as possible or it wouldn't look right. You can tell how long a body's been dead, and even if the police wanted the same outcome I did, it might be hard to sell it to the press if there were glaring inconsistencies. At lunch, Browne had said he was going out to take care of business, so that meant he was probably coming back in the evening, which meant that *I* had to wait until early evening. At least that made the most sense, and I just had to stick to my plan and hope.

I tried to pass the time with a book, but instead of being able to concentrate on the pages in front of me, my mind picked over little things, like whether I should take my duffel bag with me in case I needed to run, and what I'd do if Browne had gotten there before me. I decided the duffel bag would be unwieldy, and that I'd just call to make sure Browne was still out. There were dozens of other ways I started to second-guess myself, but then I'd think of the money and Clotilde and I'd be able to focus on the book I was reading for another half a page.

It was just before six when I left Great Aunt Alice's house. I didn't let them know I was leaving. They would have to miss me at dinner. I walked the twenty minutes downtown to the Somerset. The humidity hadn't let up, so it was hot even though the sun had sunk below the tall buildings. The streets were still crowded with the tail end of rush hour, and the people jostling me on either side made me feel as though I were taking a natural evening walk, as though it had nothing to do with murder. I was sweating, but it might just as well have been because of the heat.

A block from the hotel, I went into a phone booth and called up to Suite 12-2. I wiped my forehead and the back of my neck with my handkerchief as I waited for the phone to be answered. At last Vee picked up.

"Hello."

"Hey," I said, talking into my hand to disguise my voice. "Mr. Browne there? It's important."

"Nah, there's no one here but me."

"Know when he'll be back? It's really important."

"Does he tell me anything? I'm just supposed to sit here, like always. Put the dame on ice."

"Okay," I said, and hung up.

I leaned against the wall of the phone booth. I could feel the blood throb in my neck, and I was sweating like crazy, my whole undershirt soaked, large dark patches under my arms, the back of the shirt sticking to me. And it wasn't just because it was hot.

I took a deep breath and pulled open the phone booth door, and with that I shut my mind right off. I was only concerned with the physical.

I went by way of the back alley, just like Vee had taught me, and I walked the twelve flights of stairs too, which was just about enough to kill me, but somehow I made it, and the next thing I was standing outside Suite 12-2,

lightheaded and with sweat running down my face. I slid
the key into the lock, turned it, and opened the door.

There was no sound coming from within. I stepped
inside, and closed the door silently behind me, easing it
into its frame with the door handle still turned, so that
there was no click when the door closed all the way. I
released the handle. There was no one in the living room
or dining space. A bottle of champagne sat at the head of
the dining room table closest to the door. I picked it up
by instinct, thinking it would make a good weapon, and
continued on, the weight of the bottle a comforting heft
in my hand.

The brief hall to the bedrooms—there were two—was
dark, and there didn't seem to be any light coming from
either of the rooms. In the first, I could just make out two
twin-sized beds fit tightly to either side of a nightstand, a
setup that filled the whole room. That made the other
bedroom Browne's, which was where Vee had to be.

I made a little sound, brushing against the wall, to give
some indication that I was coming. That way she might
come to greet me. It wouldn't do to have her in the bed,
if that's where she was waiting.

I stepped into the room. A blade of light came from
the bathroom through the slightly cracked-open door.
The bedroom it illuminated was almost indentical to the
one we had had downstairs—bed, nightstand, armoire,
vanity—except this room was twice the size, which left
space for some reclining chairs, a couch, and a coffee
table. Vee was in the bathroom, the water in the sink
running.

I hurried along to the other side of the bathroom door,

where I pressed myself against the wall. I held the champagne bottle upside down by the neck, as though it were a club.

The bathroom door opened. Vee strode out for the bed where I could see she'd left her purse—almost too perfect.

I took one step towards her.

She heard me and turned, and I slammed the bottle into the side of her face, right where the bruise from Browne's attack was fading. She staggered, and gave almost a skip hop, reaching out to steady herself on the bed, which she missed, but managed to continue standing. The sound the bottle had made was almost the same as the thud of Joe's head hitting the cabinet, but with a metallic ring to it as well. Before I could get my head around the idea that this was Vee, the woman I had slept with for more nights than not in the past year and a half —but I was a pimp; and she was a whore—I brought the bottle back up into her face, breaking her nose, and she tripped backwards now, falling against the bed, but sliding down to the floor.

The sound of bubbles escaped her with each breath, like sipping up the final bit of soda through a straw. "Whh… Shhh… Wh…" They were noises, but it was unclear if it was a voluntary attempt at speech. I was heaving, and I dropped the bottle to the floor. Then Vee started to move, to try to get up. She shot one foot out and dragged it along as though trying to catch at something. I knew I needed to finish her before she could get her senses in order, and it had to be with my hands.

There was blood on her face. I took a moment to roll

up my sleeves. Then I gripped her around the neck. It was so small, so easy to get my hands around, so soft, pliable, and I made myself squeeze, leaning my whole weight into her, forcing her head back against the bed, which gave me a support to push her against. Her legs jerked again, and her hands reached up trying to get at me, but in that position, she couldn't even reach as far as my shoulders. The sound coming from her faded into a staccato cough. I felt something hard give way in her throat. She stopped moving, but I kept leaning on her throat, unable to raise myself. I was certain already that I'd made a mistake. That Joe had been bad enough. That I didn't need anything more than Joe on me. And this was worse, much worse. There was all that time, and the sounds she was making, and her neck giving way. This was more than I could bear.

I was able to get myself to let go eventually, and I leaned against the bed, trying to bring my breathing back to a normal rate, ignoring as best I could the throbbing pain in my head. Still leaning over, I grabbed Vee's handbag. It was heavy, like it should be. That was good. I unzipped it and pulled out the gun. I'd never fired a live round, but I'd been taught to shoot blanks by an effects man out in Hollywood, so I knew the basics of how the thing worked. I dropped the bag, trying to approximate where Vee would have dropped it if she'd grabbed it while being strangled.

I stepped aside so the light from the bathroom could show me the scene. She was in almost the same position that Joe had been in. I smudged the champagne bottle as much as I could in case of fingerprints. There really wasn't much blood on my hands or wrists. The fact that I was considering that almost made me retch. I couldn't stand anymore, which was good, because I needed to shoot Browne as though I were in Vee's position. This was going to be much trickier than Vee had been, because he'd no doubt see me before I could shoot him. I was counting on him coming after me.

I sank to the floor beside Vee, rested my head against the bed, and waited. After five minutes, the air conditioning dried the sweat on my body, making me feel sticky and cold. I shivered, and found I couldn't stop. So I sat there, gun in hand, shivering.

23.

I waited for ten thousand hours, although really it was less than an hour. I stopped crying after about ten minutes, and even the muscle memory of the jolt the bottle gave when it connected with Vee's head began to fade, so that I couldn't tell if I was still feeling it or if I was just imagining I was feeling it. The gun heated up in my hand where it rested on my lap.

You may think I'm crazy when I tell you that I started to talk to Vee then, out loud. I know it seems crazy, but just wait until you're in my position and see how crazy it is. So I started talking on any old thing, about how Quinn and I had fallen in love, about how we had fallen in hate, and all of the violence of that nonviolent confrontation. I talked about Clotilde. Talking about Clotilde, I almost cried again, but I didn't. I'd promised her so much and I had failed at everything every step of the way. I still loved her more than anything, which is maybe why I stayed away from her as much as possible. That's what I told Vee, at least, although I don't know if it was true. I reminded myself that all of Quinn's money was going to provide for Clotilde, that that was what really mattered. (You see, I wasn't crazy. I knew exactly what I was doing.)

Then somebody banged on the front door and my thoughts froze. They banged again, with more violence.

It had to be Browne. He'd given Vee his key and I had

the other. If I had to let him in, it would ruin my plan. I could still frame him for Vee's murder; he'd be the number one suspect. But he had the police in his pocket, and he probably knew how to dispose of a body without it ever getting to the police. If I wanted to protect Clotilde's money, it had to be both of them.

I stumbled to my feet, as he pounded again, shouting this time, "Vee, you better open up."

I approached the door, the gun lowered in my right hand.

"I'm going to beat your ass black and blue if you don't open this door this second!"

This was good, I thought. People would be able to say they'd heard him threatening her. I stepped up to the door and put my eye to the spy hole.

Browne was very close, his face distorted by the fish-eye lens into a bulbous cheek with retreating features. Another man stood behind him, squat and overweight, bald except for a bushy hedge along the sides of his skull. Two people was no good. What was I going to do with two people?

They talked, and then Browne yelled one last time, "You better be ready for the beating of a lifetime, woman!" and the two of them stalked off.

I stood there, my eye still to the spy hole, calculating, trying to decide if I should go after them, or wait, or disappear altogether. My chest felt tight and I gripped the gun in my fist so tightly that my fingernails dug into my palm.

Before I'd reached any decision, the two men were

back. Browne had a key in his hand, and was reaching for the doorknob.

I jumped back, and hurried into the bedroom, resuming my position crouched to the far side of Vee's body. All I could do was stick to the plan and improvise along the way.

The door banged open, rattling the mirrored closet doors, and Browne called from the living room. "Vee! You better have been taking a shower—" He cut off. "Where's the champagne?"

I could hear him moving around, but the sound was muffled. Perhaps he was in the kitchen.

"Vee! Get your ass out here. You better not have taken my champagne."

I waited. My heart was pounding again, the pulse rising from my stomach right through my neck, and with each beat the pain in my head swelled. I had the safety off, and the gun cocked.

"I'm going to kill you…" He trailed off as he flipped the light switch and came in. I'd been sitting in the path of the light from the bathroom, so fortunately the overhead light didn't blind me. "What the—?" Browne said, and took a fast step towards me, his hand going for the holster under his arm.

I knew I wouldn't have two chances, so I shot him, right in the gut, because that's where Vee would have shot him. The blood spread on his shirt immediately, and I shot him again in the same place, and then a third time.

He still staggered towards me but his hand never found his gun. I hurried to my feet, standing stock straight, still awaiting an attack, waiting for the other man to come in from the living room.

Browne tripped past me, and leaned over Vee. "What in the hell?" He looked down at himself. Some of his blood was spilling onto the carpet, some even onto Vee's legs. "Bastard." His voice was strained, not at all the strong man he had been at lunch, or even a minute ago. The room smelled. It could have been feces, or it could have been rotting meat, and of course there was the gunsmoke.

The other man still hadn't come in. There was no sound in the suite.

I watched Browne with no words. I needed to be certain he was dead, and I needed to get out of there. Even if his bodyguard hadn't responded, I didn't want to push my luck that the shots hadn't alerted somebody else.

He sank to a knee. There was still no response. I'd have to take my chance. I wiped the gun on Vee's blouse, stooped, and set it against her hand.

Browne watched me do it. He was completely white. I stood up, and as I did, he fell onto his side next to Vee. His eyes looked at the ceiling, but focused on nothing. The wounds in his stomach were still oozing, and there was a sucking sound there as the blood spread on the carpet, pooling under Vee's hand closest to him. His breathing was shallow, and I was satisfied.

I walked away without looking back, and into the living room, my hands empty, unprotected. There was no one there.

I crossed to the door, and stepped into the hall. I looked back in the direction of the elevators, and there, halfway down the hall, was the squat bald man. His face crumpled into a question and he paused mid-stride, before he started to run towards me.

I turned, and crashed through the fire door, as he yelled behind me, "Wait!"

I took the stairs so fast that I tripped halfway down to the next landing, skidding down several steps without falling. I hurried on, already at the eleventh floor landing before I heard the fire door open above me.

"Hey! You!"

I kept going, my steps echoing in the enclosed space.

At the next landing I looked up, but there was no one above me. I pushed on, not even wondering where the bald man had gone.

I burst into the heat of the night, which felt, if anything, hotter than the stairwell. My chest burned, my throat was dry, and my knee kept shooting spikes of pain up and down my leg with every step. I needed to get away fast, which meant a cab, and the only guarantee for a cab was the cabstand at the front of the hotel. I didn't think about an alibi or witnesses or anything at all other than the need to get away, to run for my life.

I rounded the corner, and ran towards the doorman, waving at him as I approached, and then I recognized the car idling in front of the hotel as Browne's, the one Vee and I had used to go back to Joe's house and set it on fire.

"Good," I said, between breaths, going right for the driver's side door. "Mr. Browne said the car would be ready."

I got in before the doorman could respond, and as I turned the key, the bald man pushed his way out of the revolving door. He'd decided he couldn't handle the stairs and taken the elevator.

"Hey! Hey!"

The engine turned over, and I pulled away with a jerk before getting into gear, rounding the corner just as the light changed, taking George Street uptown.

Most of the downtown traffic was gone. I raced up to Washington Hill, but I knew I couldn't go to Great Aunt Alice's—they would know how to find me then—so I continued on past the monument, all the way up past the university, past even Underwood where Quinn and Joe had lived, and was almost at the city line when my mind slowed down enough to realize I couldn't leave the city just yet. I still hadn't met with Palmer, and I needed to be certain that the money was going in the right direction.

I'd have to wait until morning.

24.

I spent the night in the car, parked in the lot of a combination garage and gas station, where an unfamiliar vehicle wouldn't look out of place. I didn't sleep much. I knew that Browne's entire criminal organization would be after me, and that had a way of making it hard to sleep.

When the sun came up, I closed myself into the phone booth at the side of the station and got Palmer Sr.'s number out of the book. His voice was strong when he answered. I hadn't woken him.

"Mr. Palmer, it's Shem Rosenkrantz."

"Shem. Is everything all right?"

"Can you meet me at your office this morning?"

"It's Saturday, son."

"I need to get out of town."

"It can't wait until Monday?"

"No, sir." I didn't offer any more explanation and he didn't ask.

There was a pensive silence, and for a moment I thought he wasn't even there, that he'd hung up. "I'll be down there right away," he said at last.

"Thank you."

He hung up.

I got to the Key Building before he did. Downtown seemed surprisingly empty even for a Saturday, and I felt terribly exposed waiting in front of the locked building. A dejection, a sinking feeling that it wasn't going to work, none of it was going to work, settled over me. Browne's men would find me and kill me, and the money would get tied up in probate for years, and Clotilde would end up in a state hospital, and the whole thing made me tired, so tired…

I don't know what I would have done if Palmer hadn't appeared just then. "Good morning," he said, his key already out.

"Good morning," I said. He let us into the building, and we went up to his office without another word.

The elevator opened onto the dark offices of Palmer, Palmer, and Crick. Palmer stepped out ahead of me and flipped a switch, and the overhead fluorescent lights started to flicker to life, revealing the waiting room I had last been in what felt like a lifetime ago. He led me back past the dark conference room, into his office, where the outside light lit the space but he turned on the overhead lights anyway. The office was dominated by an enormous desk with neat stacks of papers along its edges, and more bookcases filled with uniform leather volumes, a continuation of the law library I'd seen in the conference room at the reading of Quinn's will.

He sat in the leather chair behind the desk, and pulled one of the piles of papers closer to him, extracting a folder without any trouble finding it. He gestured with it to one of the armchairs in front of the desk, and said, "Please, have a seat."

I sat and waited.

"As we talked about the other day, this doesn't really have anything to do with Quinn's will anymore," he started.

"You're next in line as Joe's father, since Quinn's estate passed to him, and it would then pass to any of his children, and after that his parents, so there's no problem about that. Alice could try to make a fuss, but I don't think that's going to be a problem."

"How long will it take?"

"It will need to go through probate since you weren't the named holder on any of the accounts or the named beneficiary on Joe's or Quinn's life insurance policies. Probate could take four to six months and it'll cost you a chunk of the estate, but you'll still walk away with a little more than one and a half million."

And there it was. One and a half million dollars. That justified everything I had done. I'd be free. Except I was now a hunted man. I took a deep breath and let it out slowly. "I want to make out a will," I said.

"That's exactly why I wanted you to come in." He pulled out a drawer beside him, and brought out a typed document that looked several pages long. "Since you're in a hurry…"

"I'm sorry about that."

He waved this away. "I've got a template here. I only need to fill in the names, and I'll write in any other provisions, and have the whole thing typed up on Monday."

"Do we need a notary? I can't wait until Monday."

"Is everything all right?" he said, his eyebrows raised in fatherly concern.

I pressed my lips together and took another deep breath.

"It's this thing with this woman you knew and the gangster, isn't it? I saw it in the paper this morning. They said she was suspected of murdering Joe. Sometimes God metes out justice after all, although to be beaten to death like that…" He shook his head.

I nodded my head, unable to say anything. I didn't trust myself to speak.

"I'm sorry, son," he said. "Money's never a consolation in these matters, but think of that at least."

I nodded again.

"Well, don't worry about the notary. We aren't supposed to, but how many years have I known you? I know you're you, I know it's your signature. We can take care of notarizing it without you, given the circumstances. We like to accommodate our clients. Now…"

He started in on the details. All my assets—including the new money from Joe—would go to Clotilde in the event of my death. He'd add her name to all of the appropriate accounts. She was already the beneficiary on my life insurance. I had him add a clause to the effect that the money would be put in trust for her if she were determined to be incapable of managing it herself, and we filled in a template for the trust too. I made provisions for my loans to Auger and Pearson to be paid back, and then I signed and initialed a whole bunch of papers, and Palmer did the same, and he said he'd get his son to make it official first thing Monday morning. The whole process took a little less than an hour.

He stood with me when we'd finished, and shook my hand. "This business has been a damn mess," he said.

"Yes, well…"

"Yes, well…" he echoed with deeper resignation, staring off for a moment. Then he broke into a false grin, and extended his hand, and said, "May it all work out for the best."

I took his hand in mine, and gave a pained smile. "Mr. Palmer."

"Frank," he said, still holding my hand.

"Frank," I agreed. Then: "Listen…I'm embarrassed even to ask this, but is there any way you could advance me a little money to help me get back to S.A.? I haven't got it, and I really do need to get back, Clotilde needs me there."

He blinked, and there was a little flicker in his smile, but he released my hand, nodding, and said, "Of course, of course." He looked down at his desk, and slid open the center desk drawer from which he took a business checkbook. "Is a check all right?"

I thought about the challenge of getting a check cashed out in the country, and that it would be even harder out of state. I couldn't risk being in town any longer. "If you could make it cash…"

He blinked again, and I could tell he was concerned. The whole exchange felt too familiar, too like Friday nights when I was a kid, begging the old man for fifty cents so I could take a girl for a soda and a picture show. And just like my father, Palmer at last reached into his pocket and brought out some money. Only this was a wad of bills in a money clip, instead of a handful of coins. He pulled off the clip and unfolded about half of the roll. He counted the bills twice and wrote a note in the file, under the word *Advance*. Then, with only a moment of hesitation, he handed it over to me. "Take care of yourself, Shem."

"Thank you. Frank. You've saved my life." I put the money in my pocket, feeling like a heel, but feeling even more strongly relief. "I'll pay you back—"

He waved that away. "We may not know exactly how much the estate will throw off, but we do know it will be more than a few hundred dollars. We'll net this against the ultimate payout, charging appropriate interest of course. It'll all come out even in the end."

I nodded, my lips pressed tightly together. He walked me out of the office, shaking my hand again at the elevators, and then waving goodbye as the elevator doors closed.

25.

I ran then. I didn't think I really had much chance of getting away from Browne's men. He had been connected enough to strike a deal with Hub Gilplaine on the other side of the country, so I wasn't so foolish as to think that there wouldn't be people all over the country looking for me. If it had gone off the way I had hoped, I would have been safe, but having been spotted… Yeah, I ran.

That first night, I checked into a little motel just off of Route 40. Like a million other motels across the country, it was called the E-Z Motel and it wrapped in a U around a central parking lot, which was mostly empty. The clerk was a boy who couldn't have been more than sixteen. He didn't even look at the false name I put in the register. I went to my room, which smelled of mildew, but was otherwise clean, and I lay on top of the bedspread in my clothes since I didn't have any other clothing with me. I stared at the ceiling, and I thought.

What did I think? I thought I wanted to die. I thought that was the only way I could escape from the utter exhaustion I was feeling. I thought about the girl who'd been my mistress who got killed, her body mutilated, and how I had been the one to find her, that smell, that sight. I thought about how Clotilde could have been killed like that, how close a thing it might have been. And I wondered why I had seen so many dead bodies brutally treated. Of course the last several were because I had killed them. I knew that. I hadn't forgotten that. But still, it seemed to me that I'd seen too many. A man could only take so much of that, and I'd had too much. It would be better if it were just over. But it wasn't, and I didn't have what it took to do anything about that, so I had to live with it.

I tried to tell myself things would be different if Clotilde were here. If I hadn't started going with a whore, none of this could have happened. It was Vee's fault really. She couldn't blame me for doing what I did. She'd have done the same to me if I'd given her the chance. Yeah, Clotilde would have saved me.

There were no long-distance calls allowed from the rooms and I didn't want to have a conversation with the kid at the desk standing right there. I thought I'd write a letter, several letters actually. I got up and looked in the nightstand for a pad, but it wasn't the kind of place that offered a complimentary pad and pen. These places never were. They didn't get many writers among the traveling salesmen and wayward tourists. Why would they waste money on pads and pens?

I pulled myself together and went back to face the kid at the desk. He handed over a pad and pen, and I asked for a few envelopes and stamps, and for that he had to get up. He rolled his eyes and huffed his annoyance, but he got me the envelopes and stamps all the same.

I took my supplies back to the room and wrote three short letters.

The first was to Clotilde, and it basically said, I love

you. It said a little more than that, but that's what it basically said, so we'll leave it at that.

The second letter I wrote to Great Aunt Alice, and I told her I was sorry I'd had to miss dinner when I knew she wanted to talk to me so badly, but that things had come up, and I'd had to leave town, and I couldn't thank her enough, and if she could send my duffel bag back to my home in S.A., I'd pay the postage, and I'd write again soon. I felt guilty writing it, but there was nothing more I could do about it.

The third letter was the hardest. It was to Taylor Montgomery. I wanted to tell him how much it had meant to me to work with him the few times we had worked together. How fulfilled that time had made me feel, because of the writing, but even more because of him, a young man's interest and respect, the only thing an old man like me could hope for. I almost wanted to say he'd been like a son to me, but I knew that was going too far, and anyway, how do you write any of that to a man you'd met only a week ago, not even? Well, I'm sure it came out all jumbled, and I filled three sheets of paper front and back, but I sealed it into the envelope before I could reread it and make any changes.

I passed a bad night that night, but I managed a little sleep.

And after that, a week went by in a series of motels and lonely highways and gas stations and all-night diners. Every time I encountered someone new, I had a moment of panic that this was the one who was looking for me, who was going to gun me down. That kind of stress makes your stomach burn straight up into your throat and I was nearly sick any number of times during the day.

But when it finally came, I knew immediately.

I was in a diner in Iowa. There was nothing but corn all around and enough sky for everyone on the planet. Judging by the number of pick-up trucks parked on the dirt shoulder outside the diner, it seemed to be the meeting place of everyone around. Inside all of the booths were taken and about half the counter space as well. The place was loud, and loud waitresses ran through the crowd with coffeepots they never put down, even when carrying someone's meal.

I sat at the counter with a coffee and some crumb cake in front of me, but I wasn't able to take much of either on account of my stomach. Maybe I knew the door opened behind me, but when I saw a man in a blue suit head straight for the bathroom, it struck me as funny, and before I knew it there was another man in a suit sitting beside me. I'd never seen him before, but I'd watched him in the movies a million times, right down to the diamond tiepin puckering the center of his tie.

To my surprise I wasn't frightened. In fact, it was just like when I killed Vee and Browne, my mind shut off and I was focused physical energy.

I didn't move or say anything, and I tried not to stare.

The first man came back, and the man beside me slid off of his stool and headed for the bathroom, while his friend took the stool he'd just vacated. He looked at me, but just the way that neighbors look at each other when they first sit down at a counter. He ordered a soda, and then he looked at me again, and this time I could feel it was a more considered look.

I took a sip of my coffee. It had gone cold. Then I slid off of my stool and started for the door. When I was halfway there, the man behind me called, "Hey, Shem."

I paused for just a second out of instinct, but I knew it was enough to give me away. I quickstepped out the door then, and ran to the car. I could see through the windows of the diner that the man was hurrying to the bathroom to get his companion, and this gave me enough time to get the car started, back up onto the road, and tear off before they had come out of the diner.

I had the road to myself for maybe five minutes, but their car appeared in the rearview mirror after that, and I knew there was no way I could outrun them. I was in a good car, and I had the pedal to the floor, but they'd still get me, because it didn't matter if they got me then or later, they knew where I was, and that was all they needed to know.

I watched the rearview more than I watched the road. They were sitting back there, barreling down at me.

I'd say I thought something then about Clotilde, about Joe, about everything I'd done, and about how bad my stomach hurt, and how tired I was of it all, and all that kind of junk you would think would be going through a man's head when he's about to do what I did, but I didn't think anything. I thought nothing. I simply saw the wide dirt patch beside the road, and I swung out into it. I swung out, and skidding sideways as I turned, the car slammed into a row of corn, the stalks hitting with enough force to break out the windows on that side of the car. I jerked on the wheel, grinding the gears, and I managed to fishtail back onto the road facing back in the direction from which I'd just come.

The other car was closer to me now, but still several hundred yards off.

I ground the gears some more, and put my foot to the floor again, and started in their direction on the wrong side of the road, headed straight for them.

I don't know if they thought I was just playing chicken or what, but they didn't show any sign of turning.

I leaned forward on the wheel as though that could make me go faster. I leaned forward and all of a sudden I broke into a grin. My trademark grin, as big as ever and one hundred percent genuine. Yeah, I grinned, and I looked for any sign that they were going to turn, because if they were, I was going to turn, too. I wasn't going to make any mistake about that. They'd caught me, but I was ready for them.

And I grinned all the way.

See Where
THE TWENTY-YEAR DEATH
Began in

Malniveau
PRISON

Turn the page for
an exciting excerpt...

The rain started with no warning. It had been dark for an hour by then, and the night had masked the accumulation of clouds. But once it began, the raindrops fell with such violence that everyone in Verargent felt oppressed.

After forty minutes of constant drumming—it was near eight o'clock, Tuesday, April 4, 1931—the rain eased some, settling into the steady spring rainfall that would continue throughout the night.

The rain's new tenor allowed for other sounds. The baker, on his way to bed for the night, heard the lapping of a large body of water from behind his basement door. He shot back the lock, and rushed downstairs to find nearly two feet of water covering the basement floor. A gushing stream ran down the wall that faced the street.

Appalled, the baker rushed up the stairs calling to his wife. She hurried past him, down the stairs, to see for herself, as he went to the coat rack to retrieve his black rain slicker. This had happened before. Something blocked the gutter at the side of the street, and the water was redirected down their drive, flooding the basement. Somebody in Town Hall would hear from him in the morning.

He opened the front door and went out into the rain just as his wife arrived from the basement. The force of the storm pressed the hood of his slicker over his forehead. He hurried down the drive with his head bowed; rivulets of water formed long v's on the packed earth beneath his feet. Now he'd be up much of the night bailing out the basement, and he had to be up at three-thirty to make the bread. The mayor would hear about this in the morning!

He reached the end of the drive, about twenty-five feet, and looked along the curb towards the opening to the sewer. The streetlamps were not lit, but there appeared to be a person lying in the gutter. The baker cursed all drunks.

"Hey!" he called, approaching the man, who was lying face down. The baker's voice was almost covered by the rain. "Hey, you!" He kicked the man's foot. There was no response. The street was dark. No one else was out in the storm. The houses across the way and along the street were shuttered. He kicked the man again, cursing him. Water still coursed along the drive towards his house.

His schedule was shot; tomorrow was going to be a nightmare. Then he noticed that the drunk's face was buried in the water coursing around his body, and the baker felt the first flicker of panic.

He knelt, soaking his pants leg. The rain felt like pins and needles against his shoulders. Choking back his discomfort, he reached for the drunk's shoulder, and rolled him away from the curb so that he was lying on his back in the street. The drunk's head rolled to the side. His eyes were open; his face was bloated. He was undisturbed by the rain.

The baker jerked back. The concrete thought: *He's dead!* coincided with a gathering numbness and the uncomfortable beat of his heart in his throat. The baker turned, and hurried back to the house.

His wife, elbows cupped in opposite hands, held herself at the door. "Did you fix it?"

"Call the police," the baker said.

His wife went to the phone stand at the foot of the stairs. "You're dripping on the floor; take off your coat."

"Call the police," the baker said, not explaining himself. "Call the police, call the police."

His wife raised the phone to her ear. "The line's down. It must be the storm."

The baker turned and grabbed the doorknob.

"Where are you going? The basement…"

"There's a man dead in the street."

The baker lived ten minutes from Town Hall, which was also the police station. Nervous, he avoided looking at the dead man as he turned towards the center of town. The rain was still steady, a static hush over everything that served to both cloud and concentrate the baker's hurried thoughts: A man was dead. The basement was flooded. It was late. A man was dead.

At the police station, he found that it would not have mattered if the phone lines had been operational. Of the three officers on duty, two had been called to assist with an automobile crash before the phone lines had gone down.

"The rain makes the roads treacherous," the remaining officer explained. "People shouldn't be out."

"But the man's dead," the baker insisted, confused that these words had not inspired a flurry of activity.

"We just have to wait for Martin and Arnaud to return."

The baker sat on one of the three wooden chairs that

lined the wall between the front door and the counter where the officer sat. Small puddles of water refracted on the tile, tracing the steps the baker had taken since entering the police station. The officer had already taken his name and statement, and now was trying to pass the time, but the baker was unable to focus. He was exhausted.

Martin and Arnaud returned twenty minutes later. They were young men, the fronts of their slickers covered in mud from their recent work at the automobile crash. They glanced at the baker, but ignored him, talking to each other, until the officer on duty interrupted them and explained the baker's situation.

It was decided that Martin would accompany the baker back to his house, while Arnaud would go in the police car to the hospital to retrieve a medic and an ambulance.

Back out in the rain, the men were silent. The streets were still deserted. Even the few late-night cafés and bars at the center of town were closed. Martin and the baker arrived at the baker's house to find the body unmoved. It was still blocking the gutter, still sending water into the baker's home. They stood several feet away in silence, their hands in the pockets of their slickers, their shoulders hunched against the rain.

They only had to wait a minute before a police car followed by an ambulance pulled up in front of the house. The medics jumped out of the ambulance and retrieved a stretcher from the back. Arnaud came to where Martin and the baker were standing.

"We will contact you tomorrow, if we need anything else," Martin said.

The baker watched the medics load the body onto the stretcher and then into the ambulance.

"Somebody needs to fix the drainage," the baker said, his mind clearing some now that the body had been removed.

"You'll have to bring that up with the town in the morning."

"I have to be up early, and my basement is flooded."

The officers were unconcerned.

The baker's heart wasn't really in it.

The ambulance pulled away. One of the officers said, "We'll let you know," but he didn't say what they would let him know. They got back into the police car and pulled away, leaving the street once again empty.

The baker could see that the water was already flowing correctly, draining into the sewer. He turned back up his drive, preparing for a night bailing out the basement.

Inside, his wife came downstairs. "What happened?"

The baker peeled off his dripping coat, and began to roll up the sleeves of his shirt. "Some drunk was taken unexpected."

These were the details as related over breakfast the next morning to Chief Inspector Pelleter by the Verargent chief of police Letreau. Pelleter was in town to hear the testimony of a murderer at the nearby Malniveau Prison. This murderer, Mahossier, was one that Pelleter had arrested several years earlier for a brutal multiple child slaying in which he had kept children in cages in his basement in order to have them fight one another to the death. On two prior occasions, Mahossier had contacted

Pelleter, claiming to have information. Pelleter hated to be on call to a convicted criminal, but Mahossier would talk to no one else, and his information had both times proved accurate. Over the course of the previous visits, Pelleter and chief of police Letreau had become friendly.

As they ate, the rain streamed down the café windows, distorting the town square, rendering it invisible.

The café was empty of other customers. The proprietor stood behind the counter with his arms crossed, watching the water run. Two electric wall sconces had been lit in deference to the continued storm.

An automobile passed around the square, its dark form like some kind of lumbering animal, its engine sawing diligently, audible and then gone.

Nobody was out who didn't have to be, and not many people had to be out in Verargent early on a Wednesday morning. The weather had been worse last night. Why would a drunk choose to be out in the rain instead of sitting it out in some bar?

"Tell me about the dead man," Pelleter said.

"We don't know him. None of my men had seen him before, and in a small town like this, you get to know the faces of all the night owls. He had no documents on him, no billfold, no money. Just a drifter. We've sent his fingerprints in to see if there are any matches."

"You get many drifters here?"

"No."

Pelleter sat back and retrieved a cigar from his inner coat pocket. He lit it, and blew out a steady stream of smoke.

"Would you go with me to see the baker?" Letreau asked.

Pelleter chewed his cigar. Seeing Pelleter smoking, the proprietor came to clear the plates. The two lawmen waited for him to leave.

"I need to get to Malniveau. Madame Pelleter expects me home."

"It won't be a minute. This is exactly what it looks like, a drifter drowning in a puddle. I just need to be careful, and if I arrive with you, an inspector from the city, if there's anything to know, we'll know it. Benoît will be too scared to hide anything."

The rain continued outside.

"Not that I think he has anything to hide. I just need to be careful."

"Tell me about the baker."

"Benoît? He made the bread we just ate. His father was the baker here before him, but the old man died many years ago. He works seven days a week, and does little outside of his house and his shop. In his domain, he can seem very commanding, but when you see him anywhere else, at the market, at the cinema, he is a small man. My men said he sat last night in the station as though he had been called to the headmaster's office at school. And he's fifteen years older than my oldest officer! His wife works in the bakery too."

Pelleter called the proprietor over to pay, but Letreau told him that it was taken care of.

"I have a tab," he explained, standing.

Pelleter made sure that his cigar had gone out, and

then placed it back in his pocket. He took his rain slicker from the standing coat rack just inside the door, and his hat.

Letreau called goodbye to the proprietor, who answered as though he had just been awakened. Fixing his own coat, Letreau said, "I hate to go out in this rain." Then he opened the door, and the sound of the weather doubled in strength, like turning up the radio.

There were more people on the street than it had appeared from the café, but each walked separately with the determination of someone who had places to go. Most walked with hunched shoulders and heads down, but there was the occasional umbrella.

The bronze statue atop the ten-foot concrete column in the center of the square watched the faces of the shops on the north side of the street.

It was cold.

The two men walked in silence. Letreau led, but they walked so close together it would have been impossible to say whether or not Pelleter knew where they were going. They crossed the square, and took the southern of the two roads that entered the square from the west. The buildings here were still a mixture of shops and houses. The baker's shop was on the first floor of a two-story brick building, five storefronts from the square. The words *Benoît and Son Bakery* were emblazoned on the plate glass window in green and gold paint.

There were several women in the store buying bread for the day, but when Benoît saw the policemen enter, he came out from behind the counter. "Monsieur Letreau!

I'm glad you came. This terrible business from last night has my wife very upset. She could hardly sleep. And we have to get up very early. Very early to make the bread. We could hardly sleep."

Despite his loud greeting, the baker looked exhausted, the spaces under his eyes dark and puffy. There was a small patch of light stubble on the left side of his chin at the jaw line where he had missed a spot shaving.

"And my basement is ruined. One day my house will collapse. You'll see. The town must do something about this. Every time that gutter gets clogged, I must spend the next two days bailing out my own house. The worms come through the walls."

The customers conducted their business with Madame Benoît, the women apparently used to the baker's little tirades. As each one left, the sound of the bell hanging from the top of the door mixed with the shush of the rain.

"This is Chief Inspector Pelleter," Letreau said. "He's come to see about this business."

Pelleter was annoyed by the introduction. He could see himself becoming more involved in this investigation than he wanted to be. He moved his lips, but it was unclear what the expression meant.

Benoît stepped in towards the two men. "Is it that serious?" Then he got excited. "Or are you here to inspect our sewers, and solve this problem? I can take you to my house right away. My wife can take care of things here. There's still water in my basement. Let me show you."

"I'm with the Central Police," Pelleter said.

Benoît became grave again. "What happened?"

"Nothing as far as we know," Letreau said. "We just wanted to hear it again from you."

The door opened. The bell tinkled, letting the last customer out. Madame Benoît watched the three men, but she remained behind the counter.

"I was going to bed when I thought to check the basement. As I said, these storms often cause floods. When I saw the water, I rushed out to the street, and found the drunk lying there. We tried to call the police, but the lines were down, so I went to the station myself. It probably caused another two feet of water, leaving that body there like that."

"The men said he was face-up when they got there."

"He had been face-down. I rolled him over to see if he was all right. Then I saw he was dead…"

"Did you hear anything? See anything?"

Benoît gripped his left hand in his right, rubbing the knuckles. His voice had grown much quieter, almost timid, and he glanced at his wife before looking back at Pelleter. "What was there to hear? Only the rain… Only the rain…"

Benoît turned to his wife. "Did you hear anything last night?" he called to her.

She pressed her lips together, and shook her head.

Letreau caught Pelleter's eye, and Pelleter nodded once.

"Okay, Benoît," Letreau said. "That's fine."

"Did…" Benoît looked at his wife again. "Was… Did something…happen? The man was drunk, right?"

"Sure. As far as we know."

Benoît's expression eased slightly at that. He had clearly been shaken very badly by the whole incident, and the idea that something more might have taken place was too much for him.

"Ah, the mop!" he said looking down. "We need the mop."

The door opened, letting in another customer, and before it closed a second new customer snuck in as well. They commented on the terrible weather.

Benoît looked for permission to go, and Letreau said, "Thank you. We'll let you know if we need anything."

Benoît stepped back, his expression even more natural now. He reached one hand out behind him for the mop, which was still several feet away in a corner behind the counter. "Come to my house, and I'll show you the flood. The water was up to here." He indicated just below his knees with his hand.

Pelleter opened the door, and Letreau followed him out into the street.

"What do you think?"

"There's nothing to think."

"I just had to be sure."

Pelleter nodded his approval. Water sloshed off of the brim of his hat.

They began to walk back towards the square. "Come back to the station. I'll drive you to the prison."

They waited for an automobile to pass, and then they crossed the street. The rain had eased some again, but it was still steady. Lights could be seen in the windows of various buildings. It was like a perpetual dusk even though it was still before ten in the morning.

They stepped into the police station through the entrance on the side street beside Town Hall. The station was an open space separated into two sections by a counter. In front of the counter was a small entryway with several chairs. Behind the counter were three desks arranged to just fit the space. Doors led to offices along the back and left-hand wall. Letreau needed to get keys to one of the police cars.

"Chief," the young man behind the counter said. "There's a message for you." The officer looked at Pelleter, and then back at his commanding officer. Pelleter had never seen the man before, but it was obvious that the young officer knew who he was.

"This is Officer Martin," Letreau said to Pelleter. "He's the one who went out to the baker's house last night." Then to Martin as he started behind the counter towards his office, "Did we get an ID on our dead drifter?"

"Not yet," the man said. "It was the hospital."

Letreau stopped and looked back.

The young man picked up a piece of paper from the desk on which he had written the message, but he didn't need to look at it. It was more to steady himself. "Cause of death was multiple stab wounds to stomach and chest. No water in the lungs."

Pelleter looked across at Letreau who was looking at him. Letreau's face had gone pale. His drunken drifter had just turned into a homicide. And no water in the lungs meant the man had been dead before he ended up in the gutter.

The young officer looked up. He swallowed when he saw the chief's face.

"Anything else?" Letreau barked.

"There were no holes in his clothes," the officer said. "Someone stabbed him to death, and then changed his outfit."

More Great Books From
HARD CASE CRIME!

Grifter's Game
by LAWRENCE BLOCK
MWA GRANDMASTER

Con man Joe Marlin accidentally steals a suitcase full of heroin, then plots to kill the man he stole it from—with help from the man's wife!

Top of the Heap
by ERLE STANLEY GARDNER
CREATOR OF PERRY MASON

The client had a perfect alibi for the night Maureen Auburn disappeared—but nothing made P.I. Donald Lam suspicious like a perfect alibi.

Two for the Money
by MAX ALLAN COLLINS
AUTHOR OF 'ROAD TO PERDITION'

After 16 years on the run, will Nolan bury the hatchet with the Mob—or will they bury him first?

Available now at your favorite bookstore.
For more information, visit
www.HardCaseCrime.com